Betsalel

Betsalel

Called by Name to Build for God

by
ELIZABETH ELLEN OSTRING

RESOURCE *Publications* • Eugene, Oregon

BETSALEL
Called by Name to Build for God

Resource Publications
An Imprint of Wipf and Stock Publishers
199 W. 8th Ave., Suite 3
Eugene, OR 97401

www.wipfandstock.com

PAPERBACK ISBN: 979-8-3852-1820-2
HARDCOVER ISBN: 979-8-3852-1821-9
EBOOK ISBN: 979-8-3852-1822-6
08/14/24

All illustrations were made by the author, Elizbeth Ostring

Dedicated to
Angelika, Justin, Matthew, and Nathan
Who inspired me

There is no limit to the usefulness of one, who putting self aside, makes room for the working of the Holy Spirit upon his heart, and lives a life wholly consecrated to God.

ELLEN G. WHITE

Contents

Illustrations | *viii*

Main Characters | *ix*

Acknowledgements | *xi*

Preface | *xiii*

1   End of a Dream | 1

2   Blood on Posts | 9

3   New Every Morning | 23

4   Under Eagle Wings | 33

5   God of Nations | 44

6   Encounters with God | 58

7   Becoming One | 71

8   Consecrated | 80

9   God's Revealing Plans | 93

10   When God Carries the Load | 107

11   Battering Fire and Love | 122

12   Mere Statistics | 135

13   Reflections | 147

Bibliography | 165

Illustrations

1. Betsalel's Anguish | 5

2. Assir's Lamb | 21

3. Obadiah's Olfactory Horror | 29

4. Following the Eagle | 40

5. Optimistic Salesmen | 46

6. Desert Encounter | 65

7. Joel's Love | 75

8. Story Time | 88

9. Everything Has Meaning | 103

10. Carrying Heavy Burdens | 115

11. You Shall Love the Lord | 132

12. Facing a Glorious Future | 143

Main Characters

Betsalel, son of Uri, grandson of Hur, of the tribe of Judah. Called by name to supervise and make the tabernacle.

Oholiab (or Aholiab), son of Ahisamach of the tribe of Dan, also called by God by name to be coworker with Betsalel in making the tabernacle.

Kenaz, grandson of Caleb from the tribe of Judah—careful, logical—herdsman.

Phinehas, son of Eleazer the priest, of the tribe of Levi, oldest of group and priest in training.

Assir, son of Korah the rebel, from tribe of Levi—quiet and serious—leather worker.

Jahath, from Judah—careful, logical, apprenticed to Betsalel as repair engineer.

Chelubai, from Judah, also apprenticed to Betsalel as repair engineer.

Obadiah, from tribe of Zebulun—curious, shy— herdsman.

Joel, friend of Jahath, from tribe of Issachar, youngest of group—herdsman and terebinth nut collector.

Mishael, cousin of Assir, from tribe of Levi—leather worker.

Abitub and Elpaal, brothers from the tribe of Benjamin—weavers.

Mikael, neighbor of Assir, from the tribe of Gad—baker and candy maker.

MAIN CHARACTERS

Jeriel, young thief from the tribe of Issachar, who became a leader of his group.

Names in bold are biblical characters. Other characters have names that are authentically biblical, but are hypothetical people.

Acknowledgements

My serious study of the complex and illuminating Torah began with my doctoral study of Genesis, and it is therefore appropriate that I acknowledge the two men — Dr Steven Thompson and Dr Laurence Turner — who guided and challenged my thinking during that time, and who continue to inspire me. More and more I have realized just how much the Torah is the basis of all biblical reflection and understanding. Although I never met him, Dr Eugene Peterson's faith in the value of story as a vehicle for serious biblical reflection also needs to be acknowledged, and greatly encouraged me.

The core group who triggered my thinking for this narrative are recognized in the dedication of this book. But this group was the brainchild of Pastor Vitalii Shevchenko, and I would like to thank him for his vision and support in developing this special Bible study group. I would also like to recognize the valuable contribution subsequent classes I have lead in the study of Genesis, Exodus and Deuteronomy (with Leviticus and Numbers always informing our discussions) have made. Those groups may have been misled into thinking I "taught" the class, but I learned much from the concerns of participants and their insights.

I would like to thank those who have been willing to write endorsements for the book. It is an act of courage and kindness to put your name on something as unknown as a new book!

As always I really appreciate the support of my husband, Dr Roland Ostring. This time he encouraged me to share the simple pencil drawings I had made as the story came alive for me. Their naïve quality is meant to indicate the tentative, unfinished aspect of the story. I hope these simple pictures can indeed say more than a thousand words, as the Chinese proverb declares.

ACKNOWLEDGEMENTS

I would like to thank my publishers, Wipf and Stock, for once again having faith in my thoughts. They are an amazing company, a pleasure to work with.

But above all I pray that God will be glorified, and the wonderful plan of his salvation that was shared with the Israelites of old will continue to inspire his people today.

Preface

This book should strictly be called historical fiction, but I would prefer to call it "imaginative narrative theology". The story imaginatively tries to view the meaning of the ancient Jewish sanctuary and its services from the perspective of a group of young Israelites wandering in the desert for forty years, and the lessons they might have derived from their discussions with Betsalel, the man chosen by name by God to make the tabernacle. For this construction God gave meticulous and detailed instructions so that He could "dwell among them", Ex 25:8. The book explores the meaning of some Hebrew words, and lessons the young Israelites may have learned directly from Moses. For this reason there are almost no references to New Testament material which now enlightens Christian understanding. The story is the result of times of intense but enjoyable studies of the Torah with a group of young adult professionals. Their reactions, questions, and observations became the base of the imagined narrative. It is intended to make serious biblical reflection fun.

Whilst no warrant is needed to demonstrate the power of the story to reach the heart, Eugene Peterson expressed its value superbly: "At some deep level we sense that the story is the only way adequately to account for ourselves and our world . . . When we listen to the word of God in Scripture, listening for what God is revealing out of himself, a story is shaped in our hearing; and the fact that it is *story* and not something else — systematic theology, moral instruction, wise sayings — has powerful implications for exegetical work. For just as words have a revealing quality to them, so stories have a shaping quality to them . . . The story is the most adult form of language, the most serious form into which language can be put. . . an appreciation for the story in which Scripture comes to us is imperative."[1]

1. Peterson, Eugene. *Working the Angles: The Shape of Pastoral Integrity*, p118-119.

Peterson adds, "The Bible's basic story line is laid down in the Torah, the first five books."[2]

Sadly, despite the illumination of the New Testament, some Christians dismiss the sanctuary and its services as obsolete Jewish cultic ritual. But this was the means God himself used to teach his people during the fifteen hundred years between the Exodus from Egypt and the incarnation of Jesus Christ. Not only can Christians misunderstand the meaning of these sanctuary services, but many Jewish people of Jesus Christ's own day misunderstood (and still do), focusing on themselves and the ritual instead of the meaning. Christians could ask themselves whether they too are clinging to old rituals instead of walking in the light of the knowledge of the glory of God in the face of Christ (2 Cor 4:6).

The sanctuary and its services clearly point to the sacrifice of Jesus on the behalf of sinful humanity, but they also illuminate the entire span of God's plan of redemption, right through to when sin and suffering will be eliminated and there will be a New Earth with God (the true temple, Rev. 21:22) at its center. A study of the sanctuary and its services thus promises to provide an important background for understanding prophecy and future events. The story ends with a reflection that not only is God our true temple, and we are temples of the Holy Spirit, but the idea that another architectural temple should be built before Jesus returns is unfortunately inappropriate.

Betsalel, the lead character, was a remarkable man, chosen by name by God to construct the sanctuary. He was a skilled artisan, but most importantly a Holy Spirit-filled teacher and leader of others. The author's prayer is that this story-telling method of presenting the profound and beautiful symbolism and theology of the sanctuary and its services may inspire many, and encourage them to walk in the joy of its maker's footsteps.

2. Ibid, p121.

1

End of a Dream

In a blazing fire of crimson, gold, and orange, the sun sank to the west. The barren rocks around the motionless young man responded in complementary purples and blues, but he saw nothing of this extravaganza of beauty. Occasionally a deep sob wracked his body, and head in hands, he rocked back and forth in abject misery on his brutal rocky seat perched precariously on a small knoll that overlooked the camp of Israel. Even in the fading evening light it was obvious he was a fine looking man in his prime, probably about thirty years of age. He had a shock of rich chestnut-colored hair, beard to match, touched crimson by the setting sun, a fresh ruddy face, strong muscular limbs, and he wore a simple *kutōnet*, a long-sleeved, full length robe made from soft natural wool, sashed at the waist, the typical formal garment of his people. His name was Betsalel.[1]

Despite hours of sitting on the hard rock he could not shake off the horror of the morning's spectacle. Moses, the gentle friend he knew so well, had been dealing with yet another challenge to his leadership. Although it was certainly not Moses' fault that the people had chosen to accept the report of the ten spies instead of the glowing accounts of Caleb and Joshua, the people bitterly blamed him for God's verdict that they could have their wish and not be troubled by the ardors of conquering Canaan.[2]

---

1. Although this name is usually translated as Bezelel, the Hebrew is actually Betsalel, spelt with the letter *tsadee* (ts) instead of a *zayin* (z). It means "under the shade (or protection) of God."

2. Numb. 13:25—14:4, 26–35

The mood in the camp had been mutinous ever since they left Sinai. It had been so exciting and fun there: hearing God speak the commandments, building the tabernacle. But the route from Sinai to Kadesh Barnea on the border of Canaan had been tough; everyone complained. Even Aaron and Miriam were cantankerous and peevish on the trip, and tried to convince Moses that just because he had spent forty years watching stupid sheep in this infernal wilderness he was not the only person who knew how to lead, forgetting entirely that it was the pillar of cloud that actually led them.[3] To the shock of everyone Miriam was instantly punished by God for her grumbles, and spent seven days outside the camp as a shunned leper. She believed she would never recover from this dreaded illness, or be reunited with her people, but God was merciful. Her emotional reunion with her family was heart wrenching for Betsalel who accidentally observed it. If only they had learned from her experience![4] But when they arrived at Kadesh Barnea the people still insisted spies be sent to view the land so they would know what they were dealing with, and decide for themselves whether it was indeed as good as they had been told.[5] The forty days the spies were away proved a long wait which contributed to the frank disbelief when the ten spies delivered their unfavorable report.[6] From their encampment the clearly visible barren slopes of the Negev of southern Canaan did nothing to encourage the Israelites that the country was worth fighting for. Completely overlooking the magnificent bunch of grapes the spies brought back with them[7], they accepted the bad report. The vote was almost, but not quite, unanimous: they should return to Egypt immediately, and for good measure stone Moses and get another leader.[8] When told they could have their wish and stay in the wilderness until they died, some changed their minds. Defiantly telling Moses what they thought of him and his leadership, they presumptuously marched off with unholy bravado and fought the inhabitants of Canaan. They struggled back to camp piteously defeated.[9]

Now, after this day's latest deadly rebellion, Betsalel saw the forty years stretching as endless, unremitting, rebellious misery. Headed by none other

3. Exod. 40:36–38, Deut.1:32–33
4. Numb. 12:1–16
5. Deut. 1:19–26.
6. Num. 13:25–33
7. Numb.13:23,26.
8. Numb. 14:1–10
9. Numb. 14:39–45

than Moses' first cousin, the Levite Korah,[10] the rebellion was joined by his campsite neighbors, Dathan, Abiram, and On from the tribe of Reuben,[11] who, as descendants of the eldest son of Israel,[12] believed they had a birthright claim to regard themselves as the leaders of the nation. They gathered no less than 250 other leaders to their side, and rounded up most of the people to watch the showdown with Moses. Moses tried to reason with them, pleading that they realize it was God who decided who was leader. But they were in no mood for diplomacy.[13]

Moses agreed to a showdown the next day, but no one expected the outcome. The 250 accomplices arrived at the door of the tabernacle courtyard arrogantly swinging censors that sent choking clouds of incense billowing across the assembled people. Whilst God had asked the men to bring their censors with incense, it was unlikely that Eleazar, who was in charge of the oil and incense,[14] would have released the very expensive and precious sanctuary incense for their use. Thus it was not the regular, powerfully sweet-smelling, holy tabernacle incense that God had forbidden on pain of banishment for anyone to copy,[15] but a remarkably good substitute. The rest of the encampment were fooled by the impressive clouds of sham incense, but Betsalel immediately realized it was not the real thing, and trouble boded. He heard the angry accusations of Korah and his company, realized they were seriously misguided, and not worth listening to. But everyone was at fever pitch wondering what would happen, and even he could not ignore the niggles of interest that plagued his better judgment.

Betsalel, now perched on the sharp rock as twilight rapidly descended, had been safely at the door of his own tent in the assigned encampment of the tribe of Judah (in front of the tabernacle door) that fateful morning. He heard scores of angry shouts, Moses' raised voice (which he later discovered was a plea for people to get away from the rebellious men),[16] and then suddenly with a horrendous roar, an earthquake felled him to the ground. The earth on the south side of the tabernacle opened up, and the tents of Korah,

10. Exod. 6:16–24; 16:1

11. Numb. 16:1

12. Gen. 29:31–32

13. Numb. 16:2–15

14. Numb. 4:16

15. Exod. 30:34–38. Although there is no evidence that this incense was false, it was unlikely they would have had access to true incense.

16. Numb. 16:4–16

Dathan and Abiram disappeared before the soil reclosed over them with a savage hiss. It was all over in a moment, except for the intense fire that suddenly came from either the fiery censors or the tabernacle itself (Betsalel could not see which) and destroyed the 250 men arrogantly purveying their false incense.[17] But where just moments before loud cries of accusation and dissent had rolled over the neatly arranged encampment, now there was utter silence. And the disagreeable smell of burning flesh and woolen garments. Even the animals were silent.

The horrific news spread rapidly: the entire families of Korah, Dathan and Abiram had been buried alive. Betsalel shuddered. When, when, when, he groaned, would the people ever learn? What disaster would they next bring on themselves? He loved God, he really did, but it had not been easy to accept the loss of all his dreams, and acknowledge his own sad fate of being barred from the Promised Land, of having to wander till his death in this cruel, forbidding wilderness, just because of the behavior of others. He yearned to meet God and to do some serious complaining to God himself! After all, he had not agreed with the masses when they howled down the ten good spies. In fact, he put good effort into trying to get support for his fellow tribesman, the spy Caleb.[18] So why did he have to suffer with the rebels and die in the wilderness, never seeing the Promised Land? It was a very hard fate. It was the great disappointment of his life.

He was momentarily cheered by remembering the incredible experience he had at the foot of Mount Sinai. It still seemed unreal, unbelievable, that God had chosen him — by name! — to supervise building the sanctuary, the place for God to dwell.[19] But now, what would happen? Everything he had so carefully, painstakingly, lovingly made, or supervised being made, would no doubt simply decay and rot while the people traipsed around in the harsh destructive climate of the desert.

He stretched his cramped limbs and opened his eyes in time to catch the last brilliance of the fiery sunset. Despite his misery, he smiled appreciation of the panoramic beauty, and looked heavenwards. "Lord," he whispered, "I'm really disappointed in you. Please show me the way. I'm not sure I can cope with this wilderness for forty years."

17. Numb. 16:20–35
18. Numb. 13:6
19. Ex.31:2

Betsalel's Anguish.

As he dropped his gaze he was startled to see rocks around him move. He stared at one, certain it was moving towards him! Goose bumps broke over his skin, and he jumped to his feet. What enemy was waiting for him out in this desert? Then seven rocks jumped to their feet!

"It's only us," said a familiar voice. "We were so worried about you and came looking for you. You've been sitting there so long and so still we wondered if you were dead."

"Hello, Kenaz," said Betsalel, going limp and collapsing back on the jagged rock with an involuntary "ouch". Kenaz was Caleb's grandson,[20] a serious lad, somewhat of a loner, and his concern for Betsalel was both surprising and comforting. Beside him were two others of his family from the tribe of Judah, Jahath[21] and Chelubai,[22] both level-headed young men. Their presence was gently reassuring.

Standing awkwardly behind Betsalel's family members were four other young men. He recognized Phinehas, the young future priest,[23] and Joel, Jahath's best friend from the tribe of Issachar.[24] He gave both of them a relieved, shaky, smile. Phinehas came to his aid and introduced the other two lads.

"This is Obadiah, from the tribe of Zebulun,"[25] he announced, pushing a shy boy towards Betsalel, "and this is Assir, the son of Korah."[26]

In stunned surprise Betsalel stared at the terrified son of Korah. His face was ashen white, in stark contrast to his blue-black hair and wispy embryonic beard. Tears poured down his face. "Son of Korah? *The* Korah! Oh Assir! Oh, God is good!" exclaimed Betsalel, and threw his arms around the lad. "So not all your family died!"[27]

"No," sobbed Assir. "No. The hole gaped right at my feet, but closed without my falling in. I tried to talk to Father, I really did! I tried to tell him not to fight Moses. I tried; I really did."

"Yes, yes, I believe you," muttered Betsalel, still hugging the lad tight. There was a long pause, then Betsalel stood back and looked straight into

20. 1 Chron. 4:15.

21. A representative name, see 1 Chron. 4:2

22. A representative name, 1 Chron. 2:3–9

23. Exod. 6:25

24. A representative name, 1 Chron. 7:3

25. A representative name, 1Chron. 27:19

26. Exod. 6:24

27. Num. 26:11

the eyes of the trembling boy. "Seeing you helps me trust God again. There's still something we can do. God is good. Something good will happen in spite of everything."

"Me? Do I help you? Oh Betsalel, I sure want to!"

Betsalel stared into the distance, forgetting the youth around him. Suddenly he remembered something, something that might give hope and help make sense of the mess. God had filled him with his Spirit to build the tabernacle.[28] But God had also given him the ability to teach. Now, he had thought it was to teach the practical skills of tabernacle making. But maybe, just maybe, he could teach these boys lessons about the meaning of the tabernacle he knew so well, lessons he had learned from Moses, and doubtless could learn more. He nodded to himself and felt a glimmer of hope pulse through his body.

"It's getting dark—and cold", shivered Obadiah, looking at the last rays of sun pausing on the mountains.

"Gentlemen," announced Betsalel, "I have an idea. Why don't we meet here regularly, and, well, just talk about things?"

"Bad things or good things?" muttered Jahath.

"Good things," grinned Betsalel, "but if you want, bad things too."

"There's so much I don't understand," said Phinehas. "So much. Can you help us?" All the friends nodded vigorously.

"Anyone here who's had their twentieth birthday?" asked Betsalel, suddenly. There was an anxious pause, then a seven-part choir of, "No-o-o-o-o-o-o."

"Great!" responded Betsalel, with sudden enthusiasm. "Then all of you are headed for the Promised Land, and you really should have someone help you understand God's ways.[29] Yes, you need to know."

"But who can help us? I'm so scared of Moses!"

"I will. When God called me to make the tabernacle he also gave me the ability to teach.[30] My mate Oholiab[31] is also a gifted teacher, and I'll ask him to help us."

The boys looked at each other uncertainly, then back to their prospective teacher.

28. Exod. 31:1–11, 35:30—36:3

29. Num. 14:28–35

30. Exod. 35:4.

31. Exod. 35:30–35

"Might be interesting," murmured Joel, at age eleven the youngest in the group. "Well, for a start, can you explain all that blood and gore stuff, like on the doorposts, and that lamb we had to eat even though we were in such a hurry to leave Egypt?"

Betsalel smiled with delight at the question.

"Yeah, and I'd like to know why we had to get circumcised. Man, did that hurt!" exclaimed Jahath, shuddering.

"Let's meet here every evening," said Phineas with a hint of authority in his voice. At seventeen he was the eldest of the friends, and aware of his future as a priest. "Yes, let's meet under that tamarisk[32] tree over there."

As Betsalel descended the hill behind the young men who rock-hopped down the slope, his shoulders were squared, and he had a bounce in his step that had not been there since the fateful day Moses announced they would spend forty years in the wilderness until they died. In the lonely hours perched on the rock life had stretched out as a meaningless blank. Now he knew God had something for him to do.

But his optimism did not last long. It was months before Betsalel and his seven young friends met again. Even the best of ideas can be lost in misery.

---

32. Tamarisk is another name for the terebinth tree.

2

Blood on Posts

Early next morning, following the fearful earthquake and fire, while most people in the camp were still collecting manna, the priest Eleazar came to Betsalel begging for assistance. His usually meticulously white robes were smeared with soot and grime.

"You look tortured!" exclaimed Betsalel, straightening up from his manna gathering, and gazing into the distraught eyes of his friend.

"It was ghastly!" blurted out Eleazar. "Horrendous! God told Moses I must collect all those censers from that fearful fire. I had to gather them all, then scatter their fire around the camp! But the men who had swung them were gone, utterly gone. Only ash was left. I could not recognize a single man among them. Moses says God told him the censers are to be made into covers for the bronze altar, and I need your help."[1]

Betsalel glanced at his half-filled container, then remembered even if someone was not able to collect enough manna on one day, God promised he would still provide for their needs.[2] "Sure, I'll help," he said. "But this won't be a pleasant job, not like building the sanctuary."

"No, it won't," agreed Eleazar. "Apparently it's supposed to be a sign for the people to stop their rebellions."

Betsalel nodded thoughtfully. "That makes sense. A cover for the altar would stop its fire burning, yet it's supposed to burn all the time.[3] Yes, a cover would indicate people were cut off from God."

1. Numb. 16:36–40
2. Exod. 16:17–18
3. Lev. 6:13

9

Eleazar nodded. "These covers must represent a blockage between the people and God. But I'm not a metal worker. Please help me! Yet when I think about it, I don't think the covers just mean people are cut off from God. They'll be a real blessing to the Levites when we have to transport the tabernacle in our wilderness travels. Dealing with burning ash was a big issue on our journey here from Sinai."

Betsalel was suddenly horrified by his assumption that God was merely punishing the rebellious people. Of course the covers would be helpful as they journeyed through the wilderness over the next aimless forty years. God, even in his punishments, was merciful, but oh how bleak the future futile wandering appeared! And even while Betsalel nodded agreement, an uproar was heard in the camp. "Not again!" sighed both men. "Not again!"

A crowd had gathered at the entrance to the tabernacle courtyard, and angry voices were screaming, "You've killed the people of the Lord! You've killed the people of the Lord!"[4] In horror Betsalel and Eleazar watched as suddenly the soft, protecting cloud that hovered continuously over the tabernacle blazed with fiery glory. They saw Moses turn and abruptly run towards the far outskirts of the camp. Aaron, however, raced *into* the tabernacle courtyard, and, after taking live coals from the bronze altar to fill his censer, began running determinedly, systematically, around the camp swinging it wildly, as clouds of sweet-smelling true and holy incense billowed around him. The cries of outrage against Moses and his brother turned to moans of suffering, as one by one screaming people collapsed and died. Aaron was a very fit eighty-five-year-old, but despite heroic attempts he could not run through the vast encampment fast enough to cover all the people with incense. Eventually 14,700 people died of a mysterious ailment.[5] Long wails of grief filled the camp for days, and the melancholy sound of grave digging out on the high plateau around the camp dominated everything.

Deeply depressed, Betsalel set up his furnace and bellows, and began the mournful process of hammering the beautiful, delicate filigree bronze censers into large, boringly flat plates. But he did his job carefully, and Eleazar was grateful.

Shortly after he saw Aaron walking with the eleven tribal leaders towards the tabernacle door. Using his privilege as a respected tabernacle workman, Betsalel decided to investigate what was going on. All the men

4. Numb. 16:41
5. Numb. 16:42–50

wore solemn, poker-faced expressions, suggesting suppressed conflict. Moses and Aaron entered the Holy Place of the tabernacle and, to Betsalel's surprise, came out carrying armfuls of almond rods. A hush fell as Moses handed the rods, one by one, to the men. Each man carefully checked his rod to see that his name was indeed carved into it. Betsalel was startled to realize Aaron was left holding a single rod resplendent with sprouting blossoms and ripe almonds!

"Come, check for yourselves the name on this rod," Moses invited, gesturing towards Aaron's rod. But no one moved. Each man held his own rod and knew the one that had blossomed belonged to Aaron. "Are you convinced? Finally?" asked Moses, and the men nodded solemnly. "God has chosen Aaron and his descendants to be his priests. Forever! Let there be no more dissension!"

Poor Moses! Poor Aaron! But God certainly had chosen a novel way to prove his leadership choice. Betsalel could only hope that this time it would be effective.

The men left the tabernacle waving their rods for all to see. "Aaron's rod is the one that budded!" they called to bystanders. "He and his sons are to be priests forever!" [6]

Although Betsalel was busy fulfilling his duty to Eleazar his heart was broken. Sometimes he saw Phinehas, or one of the other teenagers, but he always averted his gaze and tried to look as though he was too busy to hear their cheerful greetings. He knew he should keep his promise and talk with them, but his spirit was too broken, too dry, to talk. As he packed up his equipment after finishing the altar covers he couldn't help but wonder what would happen next. When he worked on the tabernacle there were always crowds of people involved in the project. It was a very communal and happy enterprise. [7] But making the altar covers was a job he did alone, a torture. Bending over a furnace and hammering hot metal had been sweltering work, but he noticed temperatures were dropping on the Kadesh Barnea uplands. Winter was coming, and he would have no work to keep him warm. He shivered.

Next day the protective cloud of God's presence lifted off the tabernacle and moved very slowly but determinedly in a south easterly direction. So, they were to leave and move on! But whereas previously the Promised Land was the bright goal to encourage their tedious and dreary journeys,

6. Numb.17:1–12
7. Exod. 36:1–4

now all hearts were apprehensive as they saw the cloud leading back into the fearsome desert they had so much dreaded passing through only a few months earlier. Yet the horrors of the recent months had impressed everyone they should follow without complaint. Nothing could be worse than what they had been through.

Betsalel's responsibility for the tabernacle, and its furniture, had long since been passed on to the priests and Levites, but he still had an intense interest in it. If the furniture was not handled correctly there could be dire consequences.[8] The leaders of the tribes had given six covered wagons and twelve oxen to the Levites (descendants of the three sons of Levi, Kohath, Gershon, and Merari) for their service. Two wagons were for the Gershonite Levites, who were in charge of the curtains and roof coverings, and four wagons and eight oxen to the Merarite Levites, who were in charge of the frames and pillars of the tabernacle and courtyard. The Kohathite Levites, more closely related to the priests, were in charge of the tabernacle furniture, which must be carried on their shoulders, and not in a wagon.[9]

So, although no longer responsible, Betsalel could not resist checking the packaged tabernacle, partly because he loved the beautiful colors that God had designed for the furniture wrappings.[10] The gold-covered ark, with its solid-gold cherubim standing over the solid-gold mercy seat lid, was first carefully "clothed", as the Torah expressed it, in the stunning cherubim-embroidered inner veil of the sanctuary, then covered with waterproof skins. Finally, it was draped with a beautiful violet-blue outer covering, making it very conspicuous at the center of the marching throng.[11] The other colored wrapping-cloths were hidden under protective waterproof skins, but if he was lucky a small piece of color might be visible: violet-blue[12] for both the small golden altar of incense and solid gold seven-branched candlestick, and scarlet[13] for the table for the bread of the presence, although all the utensils of this table were first wrapped in

8. Robert Alter comments that "transportation of the sanctuary from place to place, its disassembling and reassembling, was a moment of acute peril for which our passage makes elaborate provision," p 699.

9. Numb. 7:1–9

10. For details of the tabernacle furniture, see Exod. 25:10–40, 27:1–8, 30:1–10.

11. Numb.4:5–6

12. This colour, *tekeleth*, is the same as that used in the garments of the high priest, and although usually translated as "blue" probably had a violet tint, making it especially beautiful.

13. Scarlet, *sani*, is the colour noted in Is.1:18, referring to the sins of Israel.

violet-blue cloth. Then the bronze altar of burnt offering was wrapped in purple[14] cloth. Visually the cloths were strikingly attractive, their colors, however, were not merely pretty, but meaningful. For Betsalel blue was for holiness, and even Egyptians regarded it as the color of the realm of the gods. For Betsalel, red was for life, although in Egyptian thinking it symbolized danger, and the rich purple covering of the bronze altar indicated the expense, the cost, of the sacrifices, a color Egyptians associated with royalty.[15] Betsalel was puzzled why God had decreed that the utensils of the table be wrapped in holy blue cloths, but the table itself was wrapped in scarlet, but knew God has a reason. He watched as the priests carried out the ark, table of showbread, and both altars using their poles, then transferred them to the Levites' shoulders. The candlestick and its utensils were placed in carrying frames, but again lifted to Levite shoulders.

Having satisfied himself that all was well, Betsalel hurried to take his place in the long column of travelers. This renewed encounter with the things of the tabernacle cheered his downcast heart. As he tramped along he remembered his promise to talk to the boys about the meaning of the sanctuary. He felt a sharp pang of guilt as he recalled his self-centered, grieving procrastination, but was determined to do better in the future. Straightening his shoulders, he was grateful to remember his purpose. For the first time in months he felt hopeful.

As always, it was the eastern camp of Judah, with the tribes of Issachar and Zebulun, who led the marches.[16] Whilst this meant they encountered all the dangers and problems first, it also meant, as on this occasion, they were first to see where the cloud settled. Betsalel could hardly believe his eyes! As they crested a small hill and saw the cloud resting in the upper reaches of the valley below, it was not the same valley of tormenting heat they had endured only months earlier. Now a beautiful green vale, with ample fodder for animals, and soft grass for all to enjoy, spread out before them. A shout of triumphal joy rose from the vanguard. Betsalel felt truly hopeful.

14. Purple, *argamon,* seems associated primarily with wealth and luxury. For further description of these details see Num 4:5–15.

15. Baker, L.S. "The Sanctuary through Egyptian Eyes", *Journal of the Adventist Theological Society*, 32/1–2 (2021).

16. Numb. 2:1–9.

"It must be the Brook of Egypt!"[17] someone declared, in awestruck appreciation.

"I think Canaan has come to us, after all!" laughed another. The cheerful mood rippled down the long column of weary travelers, and boosted their sagging energy.

Betsalel was whistling a happy tune as he hammered in the last of his tent pegs when Phinehas joined him. "Hello, good to see you," he greeted Betsalel cheerfully. "I've tried to talk to you many times over the past weeks, but you were always busy, always hurrying. When can you start those talks you promised in Kadesh Barnea?"

"Keen, eh?" grinned Betsalel, trying to hide his guilt at avoiding his promises. "I hadn't forgotten, but well . . . I've been busy. How about tonight? Can you all come here to eat?"

A joyful smile burst across Phinehas's face. "Tonight?" he repeated incredulously. He was dedicated for the priesthood, maybe even the high priesthood if he lived long enough and took his responsibilities very seriously. But he was a cautious young man, not used to bursts of emotion. "Tonight? I thought you never wanted to see us again! I'll tell the others," and he ran off to do just that.

Betsalel was surprised how quickly and eagerly the boys came. Before he could get food ready they were gathered in a cheerful, chattering bunch outside his door.

"Where did you get this fancy stuff from?" asked Obadiah. Obadiah was a curious, although rather shy lad. He munched some dates and leaned across to get pistachio nuts.[18] "It sure improves the endless manna cakes."

"You can do lots with manna, just think of it as flour," responded Betsalel. "Boil it up as porridge, grind it into flour and bake cakes of it in an oven, or flat wafers on a grill. Perhaps we should have some cooking lessons! As for the dates and nuts, have you noticed all the Ishmaelite and Midianite merchants passing the camp? They're delighted to exchange our fresh goat cheese, or cow's milk, for their produce. Here, try some of my cheese yourself."[19]

---

17. Just south of the uplands of Kadesh Barnea were the upper reaches of what is now called the Wadi El Arish, biblically known as the Brook of Egypt, see for example Joshua 15:47. After the rains of winter this can be a pleasant place, although in the heat of summer it is a furnace.

18. See Gen 43:11

19. See Gen 18:8

Obadiah gladly accepted the proffered cheese. "I don't know why they make such a fuss about those melons, cucumbers, onions, and garlic from Egypt, and the fish that every Egyptian was ready to grab as soon as we caught it!"[20]

"Manna is versatile," agreed Chelubai, vigorously nodding his dark head. "My father talked to one of those traders, and he agreed to supply the camp with heaps of raisins from Canaan in exchange for our milk and cheeses."

"Really? Is that true? That's good news," smiled Obadiah.

"By the way, Betsalel," asked Kenaz, "where were you when we were setting off on the march? Everyone was waiting for you, and then you came running looking very pleased with yourself!"

Betsalel grinned, and explained where he had been, and why, and what he understood from the colors of the travelling covers of tabernacle furniture.

"You mean everything *means* something in that tabernacle?" asked Assir incredulously.

"I certainly do," assured Betsalel. "That tabernacle is very, very precious to me, I'm sure you all understand. Everything about it is a message from God to us!"

"It might be, but forget about food! And the tabernacle! I want to know about that blood and gore stuff! You promised me you'd tell me about it! You might have forgotten but I haven't!" blurted out Joel. There was an awkward pause. "I mean, the Egyptians didn't do all that gory sacrificing and throwing blood in their impressive worship services. They offered their gods nice sensible things like food and clothing and other useful stuff. They paraded their images, and had lots of incense, but none of this awful gory bloody stuff. At least, not that I ever saw.[21] Watching my father smear that poor little lamb's blood on the door was horrible. And I was so scared that maybe he had not done it right, and I'd die."

---

20. Numb.11:4–5

21. For information on the cultic of Egypt, see https://www.ucl.ac.uk/museums-static/digitalegypt/religion/dailycult.html, 9 July 2021; https://oxford.universitypress scholarship.com/view/10.1093/acprof:oso/9780199738960.001.0001/acprof-9780199738960-chapter-3, 9 July 2021. Egyptians were, as is well-known, fixated on death and preserving existence after death.

"Yeah," agreed Obadiah, shuddering. "It was hideous! After having to keep the lamb for four days we had to kill it and eat it whole![22] I shudder even to think of it lying on the table!"

"Perhaps before I try to help you with that, we should start with something simple," suggested Betsalel. "When we arrived here this evening, who knew where to go to pitch their tent?"

"What do you mean?" asked Chelubai. "What's that got to do with gore? I just went where Father told me."

"Well, did your father have to argue with anyone, or fight for a place, or anything like that?"

"Of course not! We all know our place. Now, I'm from the tribe of Judah like you are, so we know we're here on the eastern side of the tabernacle, in front of the entrance. And the people from Issachar and Zebulun camp beside us."

"Good. But what about you, Assir? Did your family have to fight for a place?"

Assir laughed. "I'm on to you!" he grinned. "You're reminding us that everyone has their place in this camp. It's very orderly."[23]

Betsalel smiled delightedly. "You *are* on to me!" he grinned, "But there's something else that I wanted you to notice. What's in the middle of the camp, even when we march?"

"The tabernacle of God!" shouted all the boys.[24]

"Right! Never forget that. Whenever you are puzzling about something God has asked us to do, remember it's always teaching us something about himself, because he is the center of our lives. Keep your focus on God. The tabernacle is all about God."

"Interesting," admitted Joel, reluctantly. "I just hope you have a good explanation for the gore!"

"And circumcision," reminded Jahath. "What's that got to do with God being in the middle?"

Betsalel smiled again, but appeared to go off on another tangent. "Who knows their family history?" he asked, while his guests frowned in embarrassment. Both Jahath and Kenaz, who were careful, logical young men, wondered if Betsalel could think rationally, and muttered, "What's that got to do with gore, and circumcision?" There was an awkward pause.

22. Exodus 12:3–9
23. Numb. 2:1–34
24. Numb. 2:1,17; 5:3

"I know a bit," said Phinehas cautiously, anxious to cooperate and avoid bickering. "God called Abraham, and promised he would be father of a great nation.[25] It took a while for that to happen, but it did, and now we're stuck in this desert!"

"Being stuck here is our fault. I hope you all know we were the ones who refused to go into Canaan, and chose to accept the cowardly spies' advice. Anyway, do you know what God asked Abraham to do with his son Isaac?"

Assir looked uncertainly at Phinehas. "Can you remember what great-grandmother Jochebed used to tell us? Something horrible about offering him as a sacrifice." He shuddered.

"That's true," agreed Betsalel, "God did ask him to do that. But remember the best part? God provided a ram as a substitute for Isaac."[26]

"Yeah, now I remember," said Phinehas, relaxing. "Isaac must have been very relieved!"

"And I bet his father was, too," laughed Jahath, still wondering what Betsalel's drift was.

"I'm sure Abraham and Isaac were both very relieved and grateful. Now, do any of you know what blood means?" probed Betsalel. All eyes looked down, and no one spoke.

"Oh, no! He's off on another tangent!" whispered Kenaz to Jahath. "I guess we better stick around to be polite about his meal, but I can't stand his waffling. Phinehas was sure he could tell us wonderful things, but I doubt it!"

Finally Chelubai filled the awkward silence and muttered, "It's not nice, I know that much! Just a small bit of blood makes a big mess! It covers everything!"

"It sure does," agreed Betsalel calmly. "Well, do any of you remember hearing about Noah, the man who survived that terrible flood?" Several of the lads nodded. "After that ordeal, as he was leaving the ship he'd built to God's specifications,[27] God told him he could eat animals, because there was nothing else for them to eat, but he must never, ever, eat the blood

---

25. Gen 12:1–3
26. Gen 22:1–19
27. Gen.6:14–16

because blood represented the life of the animal.[28] That's why we never eat the blood of any animal.[29]"

"I've got it! I've got it!" shouted Joel triumphantly, pounding his knees with his fists, and then clapping joyfully. "That gory blood on the posts means someone was giving us life! That blood meant we got life, but those poor Egyptians didn't get life because they didn't have the blood. All their first born died, even their animals. But I didn't die because Father put blood on the door!"[30]

"You *have* got it, Joel," grinned Betsalel, "But where did that blood come from?"

"The lamb," said Kenaz, sullenly. "That poor lamb had to die for me! That's not fair!"

"Exactly. Just like the ram died for Isaac. Something, or someone has to die to give us life. I don't know exactly what that something finally will be, but God will reveal all in his good time. I can't possibly imagine God dying for us, but maybe something like that will happen."

"That's a ridiculous idea!" expostulated Kenaz. "God would never do anything like that!"

There was a long pause. The boys squirmed uneasily, and even Betsalel frowned in puzzlement. "Look, I don't know," he finally said, "but somehow, I think God is going to give us his life so that we'll be able to live properly, the way he originally intended."

"That just sounds like nonsense," Jahath muttered to Obadiah. There was a lot of unintelligible murmuring around the group.

Betsalel broke the awkward moment. "Well, anyway, Isaac was meant to be a burnt offering, an *olah*[31] which means something sent up to God, like the smoke of the burnt offerings, or climbing a mountain. All the first offerings people made for God were burnt offerings. Perhaps that's why Abraham was willing to sacrifice his son, because he thought he was sending him to God."

"Really!" exclaimed Assir. This idea made many of the boys, stirring the dirt with their fingers, look up with renewed interest.

---

28. Gen 9:1–6. See also Lev 17:11

29. Lev 7:26–27.

30. Exod. 12:1–13

31. The Hebrew word *olah* means literally to ascend, as in stairs.

"Hmm, climbing offerings. Going up to God, something like that staircase dream Jacob had? That's a story I loved to hear my father tell.[32] I thought it would be wonderful to climb right up to God," said Jahath, now clearly interested in the conversation.

Betsalel smiled. "That's a beautiful idea, Jahath! I hadn't thought of Jacob's dream, but you've helped me understand the meaning of a burnt offering much better!"

But Kenaz still shuddered. "I don't understand," he muttered. "Why should some poor animal have to die for me just so I can contact God? And those sin offerings are even worse. I mean, every time I do something dumb and stupid I'm supposed to kill some poor animal, and make it take the blame!"

"Best you don't do anything stupid and then you won't have to kill an innocent lamb," quipped Phinehas. Kenaz pulled a face and shrugged, still troubled.

"Actually," continued Phinehas, "I have a bit of good news that might help this conversation. Every day, night and morning, one of the priests offers a lamb as a burnt offering for the whole camp.[33] God must be trying to make things as easy as possible for us. We only have to offer a sin offering if we do something really dumb."

"You know, I have an idea," said Betsalel. "You might think it's crazy, but I've just remembered something Moses told me. When a person brings any offering to the tent of meeting its blood is collected and put on the altar. Now the whole tabernacle is God's house,[34] so this blood is somehow placed on to God. I remember when that shocking golden calf thing happened, and Moses pled for all of us. Moses went up the mountain and God showed him his glory, and told him what he was like. God told Moses he would *nasa* our mistakes, that is, he would carry them for us like we carry loads of wood and water.[35] At first I thought that just meant forgiving, and forgetting, you know, pardoning, *salach*, which Moses actually asked God to do for us,[36] but now I realize all this sacrifice stuff means God is telling

32. Gen 28:10–17

33. Exod. 29:38–42

34. Exod. 25:8

35. Exod. 34:7. The Hebrew word *nasa*, generally translated in this verse as forgive, literally means to carry. This is brought out nicely in Robert Alter's translation of this verse which reads "Abounding in kindness and good faith, keeping kindness for the thousandth generation, *bearing* crime, trespass and offence."

36. Exod. 34:9

us he is the one who will actually carry the burden of our sins. We kill those animals very quickly and humanely. But it seems God has to keep on carrying the load of our problems. It makes me think a bit harder about acting stupidly! I wonder how long God will have to do this, to suffer the load of our mistakes, before all our wickedness is removed forever? I just wish God could pardon us and get rid of the problem forever."

The restless mood of the group had gone. Only Joel scrabbling in the dish for the last pistachios broke the stunned silence following Betsalel's speech.

Suddenly Assir covered his face with both hands, his body heaving with sobs. Phineas put his arm around his shoulders, and the sobbing slowly subsided. Finally, tears still pouring down his cheeks, Assir said, "You know, I've been so angry with God. So very angry. I wanted to do horrible things to him, really horrible, and I don't dare tell you what I thought. I mean, didn't God kill my father Korah and others in my family? Yes, I've been carrying a terrible load of anger and misery. I've been really upset about all those poor animals being senselessly killed just to make an angry God happy. But when you talk about him carrying the load of our mistakes it begins to make sense. My father didn't have to die. So many people tried to talk to him. I know Moses was very patient with him, explaining over and over again. Too many of us chose to believe those grumpy spies instead of trusting what Moses and the two good spies told us. What a load of pain that must be for God to carry, especially when it isn't even his own load!"

"Do you think your father decided to carry his own load instead of giving it to God?" asked Joel. Assir looked startled, and shrugged.

"I think maybe you're right Joel," agreed Betsalel. "It seems we have a choice. Either we carry our own load of mistakes and failures, or we give them to God to deal with."

"That's a lot to think about," murmured Obadiah, shifting awkwardly.

"It's my job to get water for the family from the stream each morning, and I hate it. But now I'll think of God carrying my load of mistakes every time I carry one of those heavy buckets," said Chelubai, thoughtfully.

"Has God been carrying the load of people's mistakes ever since things went wrong in that garden?" asked Jahath incredulously. "I mean, our ancestors made some ghastly mistakes. Even Abraham and Isaac and Jacob were pretty stupid at times. Although I know that Judah, my tribal ancestor, finally did do what's right, he did some awful things before that."

Assir's Lamb.

"Yeah," nodded Kenaz, "dreadful things. Like selling his brother, and messing with his daughter-in-law."

Betsalel laughed. "We certainly can't take pride in our ancestors!"

"Well," announced Assir, only the occasional sob still making him shudder, "I think I need to go and talk with my cousin Mishael. We've both been feeling pretty upset about what happened to my family. Maybe when I explain about God carrying the load of pain from our mistakes he might start to understand and recover."

"Perhaps we should all talk to others about this," suggested Betsalel.

"If we can get them to listen," sighed Obadiah.

"Do you think we had to eat that Passover lamb, and the priests eat the sin offerings, to somehow help us understand that God is carrying the load of our sin?" asked Joel, pensively.

"Could be, but I'm not sure I understand anything enough to talk to anyone, not yet, anyway," said Kenaz realistically. "There seems to be heaps still to learn."

"There sure is," said Jahath, "and you haven't explained anything about circumcision!"

"Sorry Jahath," responded Betsalel, "I have been pondering your question about circumcision and must admit I don't have an answer yet. I promise I'll do some more thinking, and if I need to, I'll talk to Moses about it."

"Are you taking me *that* seriously!" exclaimed Jahath. "Fancy talking to Moses! I'd be much too scared to do that!"

"I *am* taking you seriously," smiled Betsalel.

"Yeah, but what I'd like to know is why does God make us eat this manna stuff," said Chelubai. "I'm not complaining, just wondering. We can get some other food from the traders, as we've had tonight, but why manna?"

"Better talk about that next time," admonished Betsalel, then grinned. "Maybe forty years won't be long enough for us to explore everything we need to know!"

Phinehas stood. "Sorry we've kept you up late, Betsalel," he said, "but this has been a really good time. Myself, all that wonderful news about God carrying the loads of our sins makes me feel as though a huge burden has fallen off my back. So, sleep well everyone, and see you next time."

"To talk about manna!" reminded Chelubai.

"No, circumcision!" said Jahath.

"Let's find a tamarisk tree, like you promised, Betsalel," said Assir.

3

New Every Morning

I t was a perfect morning, crisp, but sunny. Good smells wafted from Chelubai's tent as the friends assembled for another discussion.

"Welcome, welcome!" greeted Chelubai, as he ushered in his guests. "My family has already eaten, and gone to visit friends. They said there wasn't enough room for us all, and it's still a bit cold eating outside this time of the morning."

"That's very kind of your family," smiled Betsalel. "Especially as we've got a couple of extras today!" he introduced Assir's cousin Mishael, and his own friend Oholiab.[1]

"Wow! Did you see that!" exclaimed Joel, gazing skyward. "What's that huge black bird with the massive red bill?" The bird seemed in no hurry, and they all had ample time to observe its lazy flapping.

"It's a black stork,"[2] said Phinehas, who was knowledgeable about birds. "They *are* impressive, aren't they? Anyone want to come looking for birds with me? You have to go early if you want to see most of them. I'll get someone to do manna duty for me so we can go."

"Count me in," grinned Obadiah. "I'm sure I can find someone to do my manna duty." There were several other agreeing voices.

---

1. Often translated as Aholiab, the name means "tent of my father", and consists of *ohel* (meaning tent) and *ab* (meaning father).

2. Modern names are given throughout this narrative for birds currently found in the Sinai Peninsula. It is likely there were many more species there when the Israelites were in the area.

Betsalel suggested their next meeting be in the crags after a bird expedition, but Phinehas shook his head. "No, that wouldn't work. It needs to be an all day trip, trust me," he said. "Heading down into the Brook of Egypt area would be a good place for a whole day outing." A few noncommittal heads nodded.

"Thinking of manna, how did your family manage to get enough to feed us all?" asked Jahath, ever practical. He gazed at a large bowl of manna porridge, and a huge pile of girdle cakes waiting for them to enjoy. Beside the girdle cakes was a small, precious jar of honey which Chelubai proudly explained his mother had gathered from a bee's honey comb she found. "I really expected you'd ask us to contribute our share of manna," added Jahath.

"I confess I thought of that. But it's amazing, it was just like Moses said — manna doesn't run out. We gathered as much as possible, but as we cooked for you it just kept on coming! There's plenty for you all!" Chelubai gestured that his guests be seated on the soft camel hair rug spread on the tent floor. The porridge was served with salt[3] and fresh goat's milk, the girdle cakes with a choice of raisin mash, almond and spice *dukkah,* fresh cheese curds, and of course the precious honey. There was plenty of miraculous rock-born crystal-clear water.[4] They agreed it was a delicious meal.

"We did it!" announced Assir as he finished his last mouthful, and all except Betsalel frowned in puzzlement.

"Tell them about it," urged Betsalel. "I'm proud of you both."

Assir nudged Mishael, who returned the gesture. Assir was a quiet, serious lad, but this morning his eyes sparkled with a joy none had ever seen before. Clearly he wanted to talk, but didn't quite know how to begin. "Start with getting the birds," suggested Mishael, with a giggle.

Assir took a deep breath. "After that talk about carrying loads of sin, I spoke to Mishael about God helping us carry our sins. We thought we'd like to get rid of our load of anger and bitterness against God for the death of my father and his uncle. So we went to your father, Phinehas, and Eleazar[5] had a long talk with us. He decided that because we were young and didn't own anything, offering the usual lamb or goat for a sin offering was not necessary. For really poor people just bringing flour is enough for

---

3. Salt was well-known to Israel, and all sacrifices were to be offered with salt, Lev 2:13.

4. Exod.17:1–6

5. Exod. 6:25

a sin offering, but with Eleazar's encouragement we decided to use doves.[6] We thought that since there were plenty of rock doves around the camp it would be easy to get some. We wanted that life-giving blood idea with our burden-lifting sacrifice.

"Well, there *are* plenty of doves flying around camp, but they're not nearly as easy to catch as we thought! The camp doves are experts at stealing scraps of manna cakes and other things, but also at keeping well away from nets! Finally we went half a day's journey into the desert to find wild birds that were not so wary. We had to have four, you see, two each, so it wasn't easy. We caught three ordinary rock doves and one beautiful collared dove. Once we had them, I admit it wasn't easy to take them to Eleazar."

"Tell the truth, man," prompted Mishael. "Once we had the doves they were so lovely we nearly changed our minds. We kept them for a couple of days, but that was really dumb because it just made it harder to take them to the tabernacle. But eventually we did what we knew we should, and Eleazar was so kind."

"Yeah, before we had too much time to think he asked us to put our hands on the birds and confess our mistakes. Then he quickly twisted the poor birds' necks, the two that were for the sin offering, and applied their blood to the altar. The other two were for the burnt offering, and I'm so glad you explained what that meant, Betsalel. Eleazar said that adding a burnt offering to a sin offering showed we were really serious about what we were doing."

"I hope you don't mind," said Phinehas softly. "Father told me about you both. He was weeping when he shared, which really surprised me. He said he had hated doing these offerings, but when you boys talked to him about God carrying the load and giving life suddenly everything changed for him. He told me you were both crying when you arrived at the tabernacle gateway, but looked very peaceful when you left, like you both do now. Actually, Father has had his own load of suffering and anger against God because of the death of his two brothers, Nadab and Abihu.[7] He's planning to talk to Aaron and see if he can do what you boys did, but in his case it will have to be a bull that he offers.[8] So no fun in the desert hunting birds!"

6. Lev 5:7–13
7. Lev 10:1–11.
8. Lev 4:2–3

"Oh wow! A bull! They're incredibly expensive! Is that because he's a priest?" said Assir. Then he admitted, "It was me who was crying, Mishael was braver." But Mishael grinned, and added, "I just cried quietly, that's all."

"Well, was it worth all the effort?" asked Kenaz, adding accusingly, "I mean, those poor little birds! How could you do it to them!"

"Yeah, I really feel as though a huge load has fallen off me." responded Mishael. "You know, it made me decide I really am going to try very hard to watch myself so that I don't have to ask an innocent bird to die for me. But I'll never forget those beautiful creatures that suffered for my sake. They did not die in vain."

"They didn't," said Oholiab who had been very pensive up till then. "Betsalel and I had a good talk about all that sacrifice stuff, and we both agreed that talking with you lads has been very helpful to us. So, can I join your little group?"

"Of course!" shouted everyone unanimously.

"Am I included too?" asked Mishael, a little plaintively, for which he received several cheerful back thumps.

"Well," began Chelubai, "if the learned company remembers, it was my idea to meet today, because I wanted to talk about manna."

"What's left to say," laughed Oholiab, "after you've given us such a princely repast! Let's all agree it's great stuff, and that's the end of the story."

He was greeted with smiles and giggles.

"I talked to my father about manna," said Joel, tentatively, when the giggles ceased, "and he said it's to help us remember we're totally dependent on God."

"Yeah, but surely we know that from everything that's happened to us. I mean, we'd never have got out of Egypt if it hadn't been for God and all those plagues and things. Even though old Pharaoh was scared of us because there were so many of us compared with his Egyptians,[9] they were the ones with all the military hardware. They could've wiped us out if they tried. Well, yeah, he did try. I mean, we boys were all supposed to be killed off. Those two midwives were heroic women.[10] Isn't it funny, everyone knows the names of those amazing women, Puah and Shiphrah, but we never bother to give Pharaoh a name! I thought it was very funny that Pharaoh made us work so hard, because did you ever see an Egyptian with muscles like the most ordinary Israelite has? Without knowing or understanding

9. Exod.1:8–10
10. Exod.1:15–22.

he was priming us to be fit enough to walk around this desert!" Obadiah laughed gleefully.

"Remember going through the Red Sea?" added Kenaz. "That was really scary. Yet when we got to the other side, and the water came crashing down on that huge Egyptian army, I knew it had to be God that got us out of Egypt. Wow! Did I enjoy singing that song with Moses!"[11]

"But most people have very short memories!" frowned Phinehas. "They moaned about water—or lack of it. They moaned about no food. In short, they just moaned, about everything!"

"If you ask me they still are," mumbled Jahath, angrily. "If they hadn't moaned so much we wouldn't be stuck in this desert now!"

"I think," said Betsalel slowly, "that it's true that God wants us to re-member him every day. There's no doubt he's done incredible things for us, but he wants us to know he's there doing the ordinary things as well the big dramas. Nobody forgot God when we came through the Red Sea, but how soon we all forgot when we ran out of water, and worse, when we thought we had to do something for ourselves when we heard the spies' report. If we'd remembered it was God who got us out of Egypt, fed us and watered us, and even helped us with those mean Amalekites,[12] we wouldn't be in this desert now."

"Those Amalekites were mean. They didn't just attack us like proper soldiers, they attacked the weak and sick and tired ones at the end of our marching column. But wasn't it fun to watch Aaron and Hur holding up Moses' hands, and see Joshua and his army win!" Mishael grinned mischie-vously. "Betsalel, you must have been very proud of your grandfather who held up Moses' hands during that battle."[13]

"I was!" declared Betsalel.

"Coming out of Egypt was very exciting," observed Joel. "But collect-ing manna every morning sure isn't!"

"Maybe that's just the point," said Assir. "We all want excitement, but God wants us to know he's looking after us all the time."

"Manna can be very exciting if you try collecting too much," giggled Obadiah. "I hate to admit this, but I was one of the dumbos who did just that the first day we got manna. I figured I could improve on the silly idea of having to get up early every day, and I collected a huge basket of manna, at

11. Exod. 14:5—15:21.

12. Exod. 17:8–16

13. Exod. 17:12

least ten *omers*. I mean, Moses was very clear we must only collect enough for one day, but I was just a smarty pants. Oh boy, did it stink the next morning!! My father was furious with me. So I had to get rid of it, all by myself. Just think of walking to the farthest part of camp, all by yourself, with a stinking load of wormy manna! Every fly in the camp was swarming around me! It was so foul I couldn't eat manna (or anything much to be honest) for about a week. But I did learn."[14]

The others laughed at Obadiah's honest story. Both Joel and Kenaz admitted that in Egyptian-work-fashion they had nearly done the same.

"My grandmother's old and her joints don't work well. So that first day I tried to do the decent thing and collect double for her. I thought she would think I was her best grandson instead of that silly kid brother of mine. My *omer* basket was packed with manna, and she had barely half filled hers. But by the time we got back to the tent, my basket looked exactly the same as hers, and it's been like that ever since, although I'm sure she's collecting even less now than she did back then. So this manna business has to be more than just God looking after us. It has to be about caring, and looking after the needy, and equality, and especially not being greedy and taking more than you need." Chelubai paused for breath. "Look, I have to admit I was worried about you all coming for breakfast. Our whole family tried to collect more than usual, but I know the supply of manna just went on and on, and you'll all agree we've had plenty." All heads nodded.

"I wish the manna principle had worked when we were gathering straw in Egypt," laughed Assir. "Old Pharaoh sure didn't provide for our needs!" Everyone chuckled.

"I talked to Moses about the manna," began Betsalel.

"Moses!" gasped Joel. "Aren't you scared of him?"

Betsalel smiled. "Remember, he's my great uncle.[15] And he was my boss when we worked on the tabernacle. I know him very well. He's the nicest and meekest man you could ever meet."[16]

"My uncle too!" declared Phinehas proudly.

---

14. Exod. 16:19–20

15. Jewish tradition suggests that Hur, the grandfather of Betsalel (see Exod. 31:2), was married to Miriam, sister of Moses. See Josephus *Antiquities of the Jews*, p 68. This seems more plausible than the other tradition that Hur was the son of Miriam.

16. Numb.12:3

Obadiah's Olfactory Horror.

"So we are a select group," laughed Betsalel. "Actually, I'm planning to get Moses to talk to us all one day, but I have to pick a time when he isn't busy. So far I haven't found a good time. He's still spending lots of time talking to unhappy people and getting them to see God is our real leader." Several eyes grew round with awe at the sheer audacity of speaking with their great leader. "But, to get back to the topic of manna, yes, manna is more than just food and God providing for us. It's all of those things you suggested, Chelubai, but more. Now, who knows how this world began?"

Several hands were cautiously raised, but only Phinehas answered confidently. "My father Eleazar has been drilling me on this. I think he's been getting lessons from either Moses or Aaron. Anyway, Father told me God spoke the world into existence, and made everything from nothing in just six days.[17] So, we all come from God. We owe everything to God. But here's the tragedy, and what's new? Adam and Eve, the first humans, didn't listen to God, but chose to do things their own way and that's why we're in this pickle of grumbling and trouble. Instead of remembering God is God, they listened to that snake and thought they could become just as good as God himself. All I can say is, if we're as good as God like the serpent promised, something is very wrong because we don't seem to be able to do much good for ourselves!"[18]

"You've been listening well, Phinehas," smiled Betsalel. "Was there anything special that we still have from God's creation?"

He was greeted with nine blank faces, until suddenly Joel jumped up and shouted, "I know! I know! It's that Sabbath! Manna teaches us about the Sabbath!"

"Exactly!" Betsalel's face beamed with satisfaction. "So every week manna teaches us God's double blessing of the Sabbath."

"Hey, do you think the Sabbath is about putting God in the middle of our lives, like he is in the camp?" asked Kenaz.

Betsalel grinned. "You boys are pretty smart! Of course that's what it's all about!"

"And I thought it was just a rule," sighed Obadiah.

"I did too, until I talked to Moses," replied Betsalel encouragingly. "But the Sabbath idea gets better. Remember when Moses came back to Egypt? The whole nation of Israel was buzzing. The oldies remembered Moses had

---

17. Genesis chapters 1 and 2.

18. Genesis chapter 3

been a prince in Egypt, adopted by none other than Pharaoh's daughter.[19] They remembered that Moses was a bit of a hot head, and had killed an Egyptian slave supervisor, and Pharaoh put a price on his head so he had to flee, into this wilderness apparently.[20] They were very surprised when he came back to Egypt. He sported that trademark flowing white beard, so maybe he thought he was well disguised. He talked to our elders and told them he'd met God in the wilderness while looking after sheep, and God told him to come back and lead us all out of Egypt."

"Tell us how he met God," pleaded Kenaz.

"That's one of the things I'm going to get him to tell you himself," smiled Betsalel. "But anyway, I think you all know he didn't worry about disguise or anything after he met with God. He just marched right into Pharaoh's court and demanded he let our people go!"

Joel fidgeted. "What's that got to do with manna?" he asked irritably.

"Well, Joel, that's the exciting thing Moses told me! Apparently when he first went to Pharaoh he asked could we all make a *chagag*, a pilgrimage, into the desert to worship God so we could *zabach*, that is, to sacrifice, which, as you'll remember, the Egyptians don't like to do. Pharaoh complained about the people stopping their work, but here's the exciting part! Pharaoh didn't use the usual word for resting from work, *nuach*. Can you believe, Pharaoh said he would not allow us to *shabbath*.[21] Now we all know that *shabbath* just means to stop doing something, but for us it has a special meaning. *Shabbath*, stop, was what God did when he finished creating this world. How strange that Pharaoh used that special word. Why do you think he did?"

The young men all frowned with puzzlement, but no one spoke.

"Well," said Betsalel, "I asked Moses, and he said he didn't know why Pharaoh used that word. But he did remember talking to the priests, Jannes and Jambres[22] who opposed him mercilessly every time he went to Pharaoh. Apparently when Moses was regarded as Pharaoh's daughter's son, and they were trying to induct him into their priestly mysteries, he told them about the Sabbath. His mother Jochebed was a very pious woman, an incredible source of family history. It's likely she shared the value of Sabbath with her son."

19. Exod. 2:1–11
20. Exod. 2:11–15
21. Exod. 5:1–5. The Hebrew word translated as rest in verse 5 is "to sabbath".
22. See 2 Tim 3:8

"Yes, I remember her," piped up Phinehas, and Assir nodded. "It was incredible what she knew. Her memory was so sharp. She told the most amazing stories. We all loved her."

"Well, we don't know exactly how it happened, but somehow Pharaoh knew that resting, stopping, was part of our worshipping God, and he slipped into using our word for rest! The Egyptians are the opposite. Their worship ceremonies are very busy affairs. So, I think that makes the Sabbath part of God's manna-giving very special."

"I don't mind resting in bed on Sabbath mornings instead of getting up to collect manna, but why do we have to rest to worship God?" asked Joel.

"Lazy bones!" laughed Chelubai. "But really, I think we need to rest so we have time to think about God. It's wonderful out in this wilderness with no more bricks to make, but it's still pretty busy, don't you think? If I didn't have a rest from manna gathering I'm not sure when I'd have time to think about God."

"You know," said Oholiab, "why don't we plan our next meeting for a Sabbath? I think these gatherings would be perfect for Sabbath."

All nodded agreement to this suggestion.

"What about my birds?" said Phinehas plaintively.

There was an awkward silence.

"Look, why don't we go for the bird trip anyway, but we'll make a point of getting together especially on Sabbaths," said Betsalel.

"Now, that sounds good," said Phinehas. "What I was planning would not be very restful. It will be a good hike to get down to the Brook of Egypt. But we should see lots of wading birds down there right now. It's spring, of course, the best time to see birds. But it would be a good long walk. Not restful!"

4

Under Eagle Wings

Organizing the bird watching trip took much longer than Phinehas expected. The easy part was getting permission from Moses, a job Betsalel volunteered for as all the boys were too scared to talk to him. "It will do them all good," was Moses' smiling answer that Betsalel cheerfully reported to the surprised boys.

The problem was the parents, who proved much more cautious. It was well known that down near the mouth of the Brook of Egypt were many Egyptian military installations. Solemn promises were extracted that none of the bird enthusiasts would go anywhere near these defense camps. Assurances that these fortifications were too distant for a one day hike were only partially accepted. The area was also a favorite trade route, and whilst the Ishmaelite traders seemed friendly in the camp, everyone remembered the terrible story of Joseph.[1] With their patriarch Judah's involvement in this disgraceful episode, the families of Kenaz, Jahath and Chelubai were particularly concerned, and more promises extracted that the group keep together at all times. There was much discussion among mothers about what should be worn, but finally all agreed the short, above-knee-length, sleeveless *ephod* was the most appropriate for the expedition. Because they were leaving very early in the morning there would be no time to collect manna, but skins of water were freely available, and nuts and dates concentrated bundles of energy. When the day finally arrived the boys discovered they could easily grab handfuls of manna as they ran through the camp.

---

1. Genesis chapter 37. Joseph's jealous brothers sold him to Ishmaelites, who then sold him as a slave to Egyptians.

What proved most difficult was extracting Betsalel and Oholiab from their work. The tabernacle was long since completed, but these men had gained a justifiable reputation as quality master workers. They were in high demand fixing an endless stream of broken equipment and utensils, and, true to their calling, teaching others to learn their trade.

At the suggestion of Elisheba, Aaron's wife and originally from the tribe of Judah,[2] women started a profitable weaving industry.[3] After their considerable experience from weaving beautiful cloth for the sanctuary, they were delighted to put their knowledge and skills to good use.[4] The Israelites had vast flocks of sheep and goats[5] which of course needed shearing yearly, and women turned this abundant wool and mohair into beautiful soft fabrics much in demand, not only in Israel, but also by itinerant traders. At first they wove patterns from natural wool colors, but quickly learned how to obtain dye, blue from the indigo plant, and reds and purples from the mucus secreted by murex shells.[6] Wool absorbs dye extremely well,[7] and the women greatly enjoyed their work. But whilst there were plenty of Israelites who knew how to shear sheep, and women who could weave and dye, few could fix broken looms, shearing shears, and other equipment, making the skills of Betsalel and Oholiab in great demand. Another profitable camp industry was cheese making, and the two men were kept busy making vats for this. Thus there were few in the camp who were idle, and Betsalel and Oholiab were at the beck and call of all these busy people who needed their help.

But finally everything was organized, and the great day arrived. At the last minute Oholiab offered to stay behind to deal with some unexpected urgent mending problems, but the others set off cheerfully.

2. Exod. 6:23, Numb. 2:3.

3. This is conjecture based on rational indications. The assumption that the Israelites did nothing for forty years is not reasonable.

4. Exod. 35:25–26.

5. See Gen 13: 2–6, 38:12, 47:1–3. Sheep shearing and wool weaving are very old industries, going back many thousands of years in the Mediterranean area, see https://en.wikipedia.org/wiki/Sheep_shearing

6. Indigo plants, giving blue dye, were known to the ancient Mesopotamians, and probably originally came from India. https://en.wikipedia.org/wiki/Indigo_dye 20 July 2021. Murex shells, although very expensive, were widely found throughout the Mediterranean region, different varieties giving various shades of red through to purple. https://en.wikipedia.org/wiki/Murex 20 July 2021

7. This observation is from personal experience.

"I wonder why the cloud settled in the harsh upper reaches of this valley, instead of down with all that lush green pasture. We're camped virtually in the Wilderness of Paran, although it is greener than when we were here before," observed Obadiah.

"Don't know," responded Betsalel, "but I've learned the cloud is always right."

"Yeah, true," agreed Obadiah.

In their early morning exuberance, getting down to the luxuriant green banks of a tributary of the Brook of Egypt did not take long. Joel led the way, leaping nimbly from rock to rock. Most of the others competed as to who could keep closest to him. Betsalel followed more sedately, enjoying the scenery. They stopped for a brief breakfast of plain manna under the shade of a beautiful terebinth tree, and were delighted to discover manna was delicious without any cooking at all, a crunchy treat. They cheerfully obeyed parental instructions to drink only water from their flasks, as none were sure whether the stream was polluted. Joel climbed the tree to see whether it was a pistachio nut variety, or the balm version, but as it was still spring, he remained unsure.[8] He exuberantly amused himself pelting his friends with small unripe nuts, while they tried to catch them. Phinehas pulled off a piece of bark and it pungent odor convinced him that the tree was the turpentine variety.

"I love these trees," commented Betsalel. "Remember Abraham met the Lord and two angels when he camped by the terebinths of Mamre?[9] He must have loved them too, especially at springtime when they bloom red."

To Phinehas' delight a bar-tailed desert lark[10] hopped around their breakfast site, totally unafraid, and a crested lark sang beautifully from a nearby rock. A collared dove even pecked at crumbs from their meal. And everyone was delighted when a beautiful kingfisher in all his colorful glory began fishing from an acacia bush beside the nearby stream.

---

8. Most terebinths growing in the eastern Mediterranean are *Pistachio terebinthus* that produce turpentine, which was used to make a bacteria-killing balm, the probable balm of Gilead. *P.vera*, the pistachio nut tree, is less common, although the nuts are well known in the region. https://en.wikipedia.org/wiki/Terebinth July 16, 2021.

9. Gen 18:1. Whilst older versions of the Bible translate *elon*, as "oak", the term refers to terebinths/tamarisks which are common around the Mediterranean.

10. There are many sources of information about the birds of Sinai, but the following site is the primary one used as it contained excellent pictures. https://www.sunegypt.com/library/bird.aspx July 15, 2021.

"We'll see more birds if we go further down the stream," encouraged Phinehas, and they set off eagerly. Joel was excited to find an active redstart, and Kenaz, who had seemed the least enthusiastic member of the expedition, was transformed into a keen bird watcher when he discovered a brilliant golden oriole that captivated all of them with both its color and singing.

Phinehas was right. As they moved into the more marshy areas of the stream they found wading birds that can be found world-wide, although they did not know that. They saw greenshanks, grey plovers, and striated herons. When Assir found a flock of beautiful black and white birds with long slender legs and upturned bills (avocets) Phinehas was thrilled because he had never seen these birds before. They saw many birds that were common around the camp, such as rock doves, crows (both the house and hooded variety) and sparrows.

Once, in the far distance, they saw a camel train passing, but it came nowhere near them so no parental concerns materialized. They met one lonely Egyptian fisherman on the bank of a tributary of the Brook, but he averted his eyes and took no notice of them. Obadiah tried to sneak a look in his bucket, but could see no fish, and whispered to Kenaz that he probably did not want competition for the few aquatic creatures that were swimming in the murky water.

Time passed quickly, and they were all shocked when Betsalel announced they must start their return journey. What Betsalel (but no one else) had noticed were dark clouds piling behind the cliffs of the eastern Wilderness of Paran. Joel was upset because he had not seen any eagles, but Phinehas assured him he was more likely to see these huge birds in the skyline as they climbed back up the escarpment to camp.

The hike up the crags back to camp was arduous. Joel, always running ahead in youthful exuberance, now lagged far behind. Betsalel dropped back to walk beside him, and discovered he had a badly blistered heel. Betsalel was prepared for such a problem, and pulling some soft mosses from under a nearby rock, padded the blister, then wrapped it in a long length of linen he had brought for just such an emergency. Full of gratitude, Joel bounded up the steep cliff.

Suddenly there was a sharp cry of pain, a clattering of rocks, and Betsalel looked up to see Joel crashing back down the steep bank, landing in a crumpled, moaning heap. Betsalel was the first to reach the injured boy, but the others heard his distressed cry, and came running to help him.

"It's my ankle," whimpered Joel as Betsalel bent over him. "I was dumb, trying to catch up with the others. I should've just walked with you."

"Can you stand on your leg?" asked Betsalel. Joel tried, but fell back into a whimpering tangle of arms and legs. "It's my ankle," he moaned again. "I twisted it when I fell. Worse, it's my good foot, or at least the one that doesn't have a blister."

Clearly, Joel could not walk. But as Betsalel looked into the rapidly darkening sky he realized they had to get home as quickly as possible before the storm hit them. How could he help the stricken lad?

"My mother insisted I bring a cloak with me," said Kenaz, pulling one from the small bundle on his back with some embarrassment. "Do you think we could make it into a sort of bed and carry Joel home?"

A huge sigh of relief escaped Betsalel's mouth. "May God bless your mother abundantly! That would be perfect," he said gratefully. "We can take turns carrying him."

Knotting the corners into handles, the cloak was quickly transformed into a makeshift pallet, and Kenaz and Obadiah offered to take the first shift carrying the patient. Joel now had a spectacular view of the sky.

"It's getting awfully dark," he said anxiously. "How far are we from the camp?"

"Not far," responded Betsalel with what he hoped was an encouraging voice, while inwardly he was very concerned. He well knew they were far from home, that the rugged escarpment they had quickly scrambled down in the morning would be hard work climbing back up.

"There's a huge bird above us, it must be an eagle!" was Joel's next observation. "And I can see lightning, lots of it, along the horizon."

Phinehas paused, looked up, and laughed. "Well, you have you wish, kiddo. That's a griffin vulture!"[11]

Joel tried to sit up, but was quickly pushed down by his bearers. "Young fellow, you can see that bird better than any of us, so stay put," panted Obadiah. Joel obeyed, but Betsalel heard the sound of exhaustion in Obadiah's voice and quickly ordered a change of porter. Phinehas and Jahath took over.

---

11. There is considerable disagreement about what exactly was the eagle of the Bible, the most common bird mentioned there. However, there is some consensus that the bird involved was probably the griffin vulture, the bird commonly called a *nesher* in Israel today. It is a huge bird, larger than any other "eagle" found in the region today, although golden eagles do rarely occur in Israel.

"That bird's still there," said Joel contentedly. "I think he wants to come home with us." Just then the first large drops of a downpour began. Rapidly it became a torrent, drowning Joel's complaints about getting soaked and cold as he lay on his makeshift bed.

"Do you know the way?" asked Phinehas quietly of Betsalel who was trudging beside him.

"Yes, I think so, but it's getting darker by the minute." Just then a brilliant flash of lightning, almost immediately followed by a deafening roar of thunder, drowned their voices.[12] Betsalel quietly took over Phinehas' porter duty, and Assir took the other end of the makeshift bed.

"Follow the eagle," shouted Joel above the deafening noise of the downpour. "It will lead us home."

There was no need for Betsalel to urge the team to stick together. They were also suddenly more than happy to help carry the bed, and with many instead of two porters progress was much faster.

"This isn't the way we came," muttered Jahath anxiously. "We should have arrived at that very steep cliff by now."

Dismayed, Joel overheard. "Please, follow the eagle," he pleaded. "I'm sure it will lead us home."

"This *is* a different route," agreed Betsalel, "but I think it's better. Trying to scale that escarpment in this pounding rain would be very difficult, probably impossible. This morning we went pretty much due west. This route is north, then we can turn east. I think we'll be fine."

They crested a ridge, and to Betsalel's relief, and Joel's delight, the vulture veered strongly right, eastward. Ahead was a long plateau offering relatively easy walking. Although rain still fell heavily, there was a glimmer of light along the distant eastern horizon.

"The camp's pretty big," said Phinehas in a valiant attempt to be encouraging. "I think it would be hard to miss it!"

"Just follow the eagle," said Joel. "It's heading to that little bit of sunshine I can see. That has to be home!"

About an hour later, when everyone except Joel was really worried, Betsalel saw the first glow of what he was sure was the nocturnal fiery pillar of cloud over the sanctuary. He said nothing, but soon after Chelubai tugged his *ephod* and pointed at the cheerful glow. "That has to be the pillar!" he

12. The Wadi El Arish, the largest drainage system in the Sinai Peninsula, is known for devastating flash storms. In 2010 there were particularly bad floods, and several lives were lost. https://www.researchgate.net/figure/Wadi-El-Arish-and-its-location-in-Sinai-Peninsula-Egypt _ July 13, 2021

declared. Betsalel nodded. "Friends!" announced Chelubai triumphantly. "I can see the pillar of fire!"

A cry of joy rose from the very relieved cluster of porters, but Joel was unmoved. "I told you to follow the eagle!" he triumphed. "See, it's still leading in the right direction!"

The rain had now eased, and at Obadiah's suggestion, they agreed to make a concerted shout at regular intervals in the hope that someone from the camp would hear and come to meet them. The ploy worked, and soon five large torches were seen heading towards them. By the time they met the torch bearers the tents of the Israelites were clearly visible.

"There's been a terrible storm here," was the first thing the greeters announced. "Lots of thunder and lightning, and we saw it heading straight down the valley towards you. Your parents were very worried."

"Any damage done?" asked Betsalel.

"No, thankfully, God protected us."

"The eagle led us home," cried Joel triumphantly, drawing attention to himself. "I'm sure God sent it."

"Hello, hello! You've got an injured party, eh?"

"Yeah," replied Betsalel. "Probably just a badly sprained ankle. He fell down a bit of a cliff."

"Hey, the eagle has settled on those high rocks over there. I can see his eerie," insisted Joel, now much more interested in the eagle than his injured leg. But at that moment only Phinehas retained an interest in birds and followed his pointing fingers.

Rain was still falling lightly as they trudged into the camp, but what a welcome they received! Only Oholiab's younger brother seemed unaware of the general mood of rejoicing. "You didn't bring back any fish!" he grumbled. He was ignored.

"It's Aaron!" exclaimed Jahath in shocked surprise when they saw the whole priestly team, Aaron, Eleazar, and Ithamar, as well as many Levites, coming towards them. But there was no mistaking the magnificent robes of the high priest. Even in semidarkness, with only the light of the torches and still-distant fiery pillar, the twelve gems on his breastplate lying against the intricately patterned *ephod* glistened, and the bells on the hem of his beautiful blue robe tinkled gently. As he drew closer the gold in his turban gleamed and the great onyx stones on his shoulder pieces glittered.[13]

---

13. See Exod. 28:2–39 for a description of the high priest's clothing.

Following the Eagle.

"It is most gratifying to all of us, and brings us inconceivable joy and pleasure to have you return safely into the bosom of the camp," began Aaron in his usual elegant, formal style.[14] "It has been decided that your safe return provides a suitable occasion for a *todah*, a thanksgiving, peace offering.[15] If you would like to perform your appropriate ablutions and change into suitable attire everything is in readiness for us to celebrate at the tabernacle."

"You're kidding! For us!" exclaimed Obadiah involuntarily.

Eleazar patted him gently on the shoulder. "We're not kidding," he smiled. "There's been a lot of anxiety about you all when that terrible storm rolled up. And by the feel of you, you will all be very glad of a change in clothes!"

"It is all appropriately arranged," continued Aaron. "Please prepare yourselves and come to the gate of the courtyard of the tent of meeting. The unblemished lamb and holy unleavened bread is all in readiness. Moses will join our joyful company after you are prepared with your cleansing and pure clothes."

"But I'm not unblemished!" cried Joel in a stricken voice. "My ankle is damaged!"

"Only the sacrificial lamb has to be unblemished," assured Eleazar. "You have many friends who'll be pleased to act as your staff and assist you."

The Merarite[16] Levites had prepared water for bathing, and the families of the young adventurers had clean *kutōnet* ready. Except for Betsalel, the awe-struck young men were silent as they assembled at the door of the tabernacle, Joel leaning on the arm of Oholiab who was, of course, deemed part of the team. To their shock Moses really was there to greet them. Unlike Aaron, his greeting was simple.

"Sons," he began, "with much gratitude to our God of love, Yahweh, we celebrate your safe return to us. May he be present with us as we acknowledge his blessings."

Not even Betsalel could watch as Eleazar, first placing his hand reverently on the lamb, killed it and removed the blood, fat, kidneys, and liver. Then, after applying the blood to the altar, he burnt the removed parts on the altar as a burnt offering.[17] The rest of the lamb was barbecue-roasted

---

14. Exod. 4:14. Aaron was known for his elegant speech.

15. Lev 7:11–15

16. Numb. 3:33–37

17. Lev 3:1–5

for them to partake as a feast to the Lord. Although the service began very formally, it became quite festive as the meat of the lamb and its accompanying oiled manna cakes were shared around the adventurers, their families, the Levites, and the priests.

"It's strange, but it's so long since I've eaten flesh that I find it a bit hard to enjoy," admitted Betsalel to Oholiab.

"Yeah," agreed his colleague. "Why do you think we have to eat it?"

"Not sure, but the lamb was given to God for thanksgiving, and maybe it means we are taking a grateful spirit into our bodies. Or perhaps it's got something to do with sharing the burdens of God."

"Both those ideas make sense."

"You know, this ritual makes God seem like part of the family, don't you think?" whispered Kenaz to Joel. Betsalel overheard and smiled.

"I thought all those rules about the peace offerings were pretty tedious," confided Assir to Betsalel. "But what Kenaz just said makes me realize God really does want us to be part of his family. You mightn't like the meat, but isn't it amazing that God has left all the good parts for us to eat, and taken all the rubbish for himself! Now that's real unselfishness!"

The others, overhearing him, nodded surprised agreement. It was amazing, shocking, to think that God gave all the best to them. Certainly, with the light of the fiery cloud beaming closely down upon them, and the beautiful curtains of the courtyard and tabernacle entrances flapping in a gentle breeze, God did seem very near.

"You're right!" agreed Betsalel, surprised by Assir's observation. "I guess God's rules are always there to help us, if only we could trust him! I'm sorry I grizzled about eating this mutton. It really is rather nice, after all!"

At the end of the service, Aaron pronounced the special priestly blessing: *The Lord bless you and keep you: The Lord make his face to shine on you, and be gracious unto you: The Lord lift up his face upon you and give you peace.*[18]

"You know, I'm exhausted but very excited. This has been an incredible day," admitted Jahath to Betsalel, as they walked home.

"It has," agreed Betsalel. "I think we'll all sleep very well!"

"Especially the parents," laughed Jahath.

Next morning when they looked down to the valley of the Brook of Egypt to their astonishment they saw a lake instead of land. Now they realized why the cloud of God's presence had rested where it did. Camping in

18. Numb. 6:22–26.

the once beautiful green grassy area of the Brook would not have been a good idea.

"God always knows best," smiled Obadiah to Betsalel as they gazed at the new landscape below them.

5

God of Nations

Joel's sprained ankle healed quickly, and he was almost back to normal by their next meeting. Betsalel had made a cage from acacia wood, softly lined with lambs' wool, which enabled Joel to walk quite happily until his ankle healed. Soon after the storm and bird expedition, the cloud over the tabernacle moved, but not before Phinehas and Assir climbed the crags to find the griffon vulture eerie. They came home and excitedly announced they had found a colony of about 25 pairs, and several nestlings.[1]

The cloud moved to the east where they camped for a few months, and then south to Ezion-geber.[2] The uplands of the southern Negev became unbearably hot in summer, and although Ezion-geber was hot, sea breezes around the head of the Gulf of Aqaba offered a pleasant change. Youngsters availed themselves of the opportunity to play in the water, and many young boys were amazed at the beautiful corals they found when they went diving.[3] Phinehas pointed out many more birds to his friends, and Joel was particularly happy when he discovered a whole new set of eagle-type birds: a white-tailed sea eagle, goshawks, black kites and red kites, a greater spotted eagle, and one day an imperial eagle. "I hope we can

---

1. Unlike true eagles, griffon vultures nest in colonies.

2. The Bible gives very accurate details about the camp sites of the Israelites on their journeys, see Numb 33:5–49, but unfortunately most are not identifiable today. However, Ezion-geber is well testified as a port on the Gulf of Aqaba, see 1 Kings 9:26, & 22:48, and it was most probably in the area of the modern port city of Eilat.

3. The Gulf of Aqaba is one of the world's most famous diving sites. https:// en.wikipedia.org/wiki/Gulf_of_Aqaba July 17, 2021

stay here till spring," commented Phinehas. "In Egypt lots of birds migrated through in spring."

In this location they also saw many traders, as men came from the regions of Edom, Moab, and Ammon, and even far-off countries like Basham, Elam,[4] and Assur, to make use of the port.[5]

Betsalel and his friends held regular Sabbath meetings, often with their families, and their number had grown to thirteen. The new additions were the brothers Abitub and Elpaal, friends of Jahath from the tribe of Benjamin,[6] and Mikael, a neighbor of Assir from the tribe of Gad.[7] Betsalel encouraged all members of the group to share what they discussed with their friends, thus encouraging as many as possible to understand God's plans. But although Jahath had several times told them of the group, Abitub and Elpaal were at first reluctant to join because they thought they wouldn't fit in.

The Benjaminite brothers, conspicuous by their tousled red hair, finally joined because they were distressed by an unpleasant encounter they had with passing traders. Betsalel himself told them of the group when they shared their story with him while he repaired cheese vats for their parents, and realizing the leader of the group was friendly, they finally accepted the invitation.

"So, tell the others what happened," encouraged Betsalel, after introductions.

"Father makes top quality cheeses, as you know," began Abitub, gesticulating towards Betsalel, "and he asked me to take some to these traders that arrived near our camp. Mother had some of her famous checker-work fabric ready to sell, so we took that too."

4. The area of Persia

5. See 1 Kings 9:26

6. Representative names, see 1 Chron. 8:1, 11

7. Representative name, see 1 Chron. 5:11, 13

Optimistic Salesmen.

"We live way over on the west side," added Elpaal, when he saw blank faces, "far from any of you guys here on the east. I'm so glad Jahath and Betsalel told us about you, because sometimes it gets a bit lonely over there."

"But you're all the descendants of Rachel[8] in that part of the camp, aren't you?" asked Phinehas, ever keen to be accurate regarding procedural matters.

"Yeah, the tribe of Benjamin, that's us, then Ephraim and Manasseh the sons of Joseph. But those E'n'Ms,[9] as we call them, are all half Egyptian, you know. That's probably why they're a bit wild. Some of them like to skite about the fact that their great-great-whatever-grandmother Asenath, wife of the famous famine-relieving Joseph, was of royal Egyptian blood, daughter of a priest of the important temple at On. They especially like to remind us that we're from the youngest kid brother of the family, the bottom of the pile!"[10]

"It's funny," added Abitub, with a twisted grin, "those E'n'Ms never talked about their great-great-whatever grandmother while we were in Egypt suffering under those taskmasters! But out here in the desert, being part Egyptian seems to make them feel superior to us Benjaminites."

"You know," said Phinehas, thoughtfully, "I think I also have Egyptian blood. My maternal grandfather was called Putiel.[11] Put is another name for Egypt, so although the name hints that he worshipped God, he sounds as though he wasn't one of us."

Oholiab, who suffered fools lightly, looked angry, and staring at Abitub, exclaimed roughly, "I've heard people from your side of the camp boast that you're the only true descendants of Israel, because Rachel was his only true wife! How arrogant! Just as well Moses put you all over there well away from the rest of us, because you'd be more than we could handle! My ancestor Dan was born because your wonderful Rachel couldn't have any kids!"[12]

---

8. Gen 46:19–22

9. Of course this would not be the Hebrew version, which would be something like "*alephimvavmemim*", *aleph* being the first letter of Ephraim, and *mem* that of Manasseh, *vav* is Hebrew for and, and "*im*" a plural.

10. Gen 41:45; 35:16–18; 43:13–15

11. Exod. 6:25

12. Gen. 30:1–8

"Come, come," said Betsalel soothingly, "all our ancestors made terrible mistakes. Our job is not to follow their behavior. We don't need to focus on our ancestors, but do what God wants us to do."

Elpaal clapped his hands in excitement. "That's exactly what I've been saying to those uppity E'n'Ms! None of us gets to choose who we come from, and all we can do is learn not make the awful bungles our forebears did!"

"Exactly," agreed Betsalel. "Now, continue your story, Abitub." But Oholiab continued to scowl.

"Well, I offered the cheeses and the traders offered some dates, but also beautiful shiny cloth from Elam. They were very interested in mother's cloth, and I was just trying to decide whether mother would like their cloth or not, when these bullies from Ephraim came up with their cheese, snatched my cloth from under my nose, yelled they'd take it, but at only half what I was prepared to offer. That made the traders cross because they wanted mother's cloth, so they began screaming at us all, particularly Elpaal and me, perhaps because we were young."

"They not only yelled at us, but began brandishing long knives!" added Elpaal. "I tell you, it was scary, very."

"Where did those guys come from?" asked Obadiah, who as always was the most curious. "Perhaps they didn't know who we are?"

"They knew, alright!" exploded Abitub. "They knew only too well, and that seemed to be the problem. They kept yelling 'Sons of the supplanter! Sons of the supplanter! You should be wiped off the face of the earth!' And much worse things too! Oh, to answer your question, they were Edomites."

"Edomites? Whatever were they talking about?" frowned Joel, now sporting the faint smudges of a beard, but still the youngest in the group.

"For those of you who don't know the story," began Phinehas, who, as future priest had become extremely interested in national history, "Edomites are descended from Esau.[13] Esau was the older twin brother of our ancestor Jacob, whose name means cheat, or supplanter, but he was given the dignified new name of Israel by God."[14]

"Why didn't they both become God's men?" asked Jahath. "Twins should be equal, surely?"

"That's the real issue. Esau wanted to do his own thing," declared Phineas solemnly. "He chose eating and hunting rather than God, and

13. Gen 36:1
14. Gen 32:28. Israel means "striven with God and man, and has prevailed."

48

married Hittite women.[15] But before we get all conceited, Jacob was pretty despicable. He literally stole the birthright from Esau, and because of that, as you all know, had to run for his life to Paddam-Aram in northern Mesopotamia.[16] But the big difference was Jacob did keep on worshipping God, and followed him despite mistakes."

Silence followed Phinehas' explanation. Abitub finally said, "You know, they weren't all Edomites in that caravan. As soon as this chap started getting upset, the rest all joined in with 'We have even more rights! We are the true sons of Abraham! Down with all you upstart supplanters!' Then I realized those traders were Ishmaelites. There were lots of angry men around us. I tell you! It was scary!"

"Yes, it's very sad, even our great Father Abraham did some really stupid things, and it's caused trouble to us since," agreed Betsalel. "God promised Abraham he would be the father of a great nation.[17] But he had no children! I don't know how long he had been trying for kids, but certainly ten years after that promise there were still no signs of a family.[18] I can sympathize with that because I have no children, although I really wanted some.[19] Anyway, Sarah persuaded her husband to give God a helping hand, and Hagar, Sarah's Egyptian maid, was given to Abraham as a concubine. Hagar became the mother of Ishmael."[20]

"Giving God a helping hand sounds a bit risky, if you ask me!" observed Joel.

"Yeah, just like happened with my ancestor mother, Bilhah,"[21] muttered Oholiab angrily. "Here on the east you're all pure blooded descendants of Leah, the tribes of Judah, Issachar, and Zebulun. And on the west you're pure descendants of Rachel, but those of us on the north are just the rubbish from a very sick and unbelievably miserable family!" He jumped up, angry from memories of abuse from other tribes. Clearly he'd had enough of squabbles, and was about to leave the group. Betsalel opened his mouth to call him back, but was interrupted.

---

15. Gen 25:34; 26:34–35

16. See Genesis chapter 27.

17. Gen 12:1–3

18. Compare Gen 12:4 and 16:16.

19. The Bible does not record any children from Betsalel, but of course this comment is conjecture.

20. Gen 16:15

21. Gen 30:1–6

"And remember Zilpah,[22] my ancestor!" laughed Mikael nonchalantly. "And look what she got, the good fortune of my patriarch Gad!"[23]

"Well, your patriarch at least got called 'Good Fortune' and not 'Judged' like mine did!" retorted Oholiab. This made everyone laugh. They began joking about their ancestral names, all agreeing that Judah, meaning "praise" was the luckiest with his name, and those from the tribe of Levi decided their name, meaning "stuck together" was the most unfortunate, although Phinehas tried valiantly to point out good aspects of the name.

After all the joking and hilarity had settled down, and Oholiab was pacified and once more seated with the group, a rather serious Kenaz spoke up. "You don't know how lucky you all are. I don't what my name means, although they tell me it means hunter and comes from those awful Edomites. Their ancestor Esau was a hunter, you'll remember. I must have one of them as an ancestor somewhere. And I'm stuck with my name!"

"Really!" gasped Abitub in sudden horror. "I'm *so* sorry. I never meant to upset you!" Kenaz nodded curtly, but the mood in the group was far from happy.

"Look, before we go any further, perhaps we better hear the full story of what happened with the traders," advised Betsalel. "It might give some perspective about the issues in our nation."

"Yeah, thanks," said Abitub, relieved at the change in topic. "Well, Elpaal and I were standing looking at our cheese, knowing we were no match for half a dozen burly Ephraimites and about a dozen angry traders with murderous knives. Then this man who'd been standing by the camels suddenly marched across to us. He was big and impressive, clearly their leader, but softly spoken. 'Hush! Hush! Hush to all of you!' he called, gently, and the noise stopped like magic. 'This is not the way we traders behave. We are peaceful men and carry knives only to protect ourselves from wild beasts. We worship the great El Shaddai,[24] the same Mighty God the ancestors of these people worshipped. Let us show them we are decent and god-fearing men, and not godless heathen[25] like the Egyptians they have so recently escaped from."

---

22. Gen 30:9–11

23. Gad, Mikael's tribal name, means good fortune, Gen 30:11

24. Exod. 6:2–3

25. Ancient monotheists often regarded the polytheistic nations such as Egypt as virtually without any real god.

"Yeah, he was nice," said Elpaal. "Well, immediately all the traders started sheathing their knives, and most looked ashamed. Those arrogant Ephraimites just slunk away in shock, or perhaps even fear. Abitub and I were left there with our cheese and mother's cloth, wondering if the man was an angel from our God. Then he came over to us, and said in the kindest voice possible, 'I see you have good quality cheese. What did you want to exchange it for?'"

"He was so kind," added Abitub. "When we coughed and spluttered a bit because we were so surprised and didn't quite know how to take him, he said, 'You've had a bad fright, sons. Just take some deep breaths, and then tell me what you want.' So I pointed to the dates, and Elpaal touched the shiny cloth, and he organized the deal just like that!"

"But that's not the end of the story," added Elpaal, beaming with excitement. "Just as we were gathering up the dates and cloth he came close to us and asked quietly did we know a man called Moses! I mean, what a question! Did we know Moses? I tried not to laugh as I said yes. Turns out he was a Midianite who knew Moses when he was a shepherd! What a shock! His name was Ephah,[26] and he asked if he could speak with Moses. Remembering all those long knives I wondered if it was a trick, but we agreed to see if we could find Moses. We both ran like the wind!"

"Yeah, and, can you believe it, Moses remembered him, and came out to meet him, and they embraced! I was shocked!" exclaimed Abitub. "Moses invited him to stay and eat with him, but Ephah refused, saying he had already kept his men waiting long enough, but maybe next time they could arrange something."

"Did anyone else come and trade with the men?" asked Obadiah.

"Yes, while Moses and his old friend were talking there were people bringing more cheese, woolen cloth, and leather sandals. But we didn't take much notice. It was all very confusing. Fighting one minute and then suddenly best friends!"

"But I think," began Phinehas with an air of superiority, "we are the chosen of God. All those other people are somehow . . ." Phineas paused uncertainly.

"Inferior! Spit it out man!" urged Assir.

"Well, isn't that true?"

"Let's think," said Betsalel, and took a deep breath. "Now, take me for example. I'm a true blue Judahite, leader of all the tribes, as I am sure you

---

26. A Midianite name, see Gen 25:4

know," and before Oholiab could bristle with anger, he smiled and added, "with a proud matriarch who was not only a prostitute, but a Canaanite one to boot!"[27]

Jahath and Kenaz began to giggle. "We've been told never to mention Tamar, it's so embarrassing."

"Perhaps it is," smiled Betsalel. "But it's true. And over on the west there we have two tribes that we all know are half Egyptian. And no less than a third of us come from tribes whose matriarchs were mere slaves, as Oholiab has already so carefully told us, and then . . ."

Jahath raised his hand. He was not giggling now.

"What is it?" asked Betsalel.

"I'm — I'm not sure if I should mention this. But isn't our great leader Moses married to a Midianite? I remember there was that terrible time when the whole camp had to wait for Miriam for a whole week because she had grumbled about his foreign wife and got punished with leprosy."[28]

"That's right!" exclaimed Betsalel.

"Got it!" cried Joel, jumping up and then sitting quickly with a soft moan because he had forgotten his ankle still hurt. "Got it! There's not one of us in this camp who's true blooded or deserves to be called chosen of God. Those grumpy traders apparently have as much ancestral right to be God's people as we have!"

"Yes, you have got it," smiled Betsalel, nodding vigorously.

"But wasn't Abraham called by God?" persisted Phinehas defensively. "I've been spending lots of time studying our nation's history! Don't tell me all those despicable people that live in those other places are equal with us!"

"Don't you think the issue was that Abraham *answered* the call of God, not just that he was called?" asked Betsalel, smilingly. "I mean, Zipporah, Moses' wife, and her whole family, were truly dedicated to God."[29]

"And Ishmael and Esau didn't respond to God's call?" suggested Chelubai, who had been very quiet during the discussion. Betsalel nodded.

Suddenly there was a lot of leg stretching and moving around as the young men digested these strange ideas. Most had been deeply convinced they were indeed the chosen of God, the only people on the face of the earth who were worth anything, and the traders that they interacted with merely from sheer necessity were far inferior. Betsalel was a good chap, they

27. Gen 38:1–38
28. Exod.2:15–22, 18:1–5, Numb. 12:1–15
29. Exod. 18:7–12

agreed, but somehow he could be a bit, well, just plain impractical, out of this world with his noble ideas.

Then Phinehas sat up. "This time I think it's me who's got it!" he exclaimed, a look of wonder on his face. "God *did* call Abraham. He was asked to leave his family, and culture, and country, and go far away. And Abraham did it! God promised he would become a great nation, which I think you can say we have!" he waved his hands over the group, and then pointed to the surrounding tents in their neatly arranged formation. "God promised to bless him, and give him a great name, and protect him and all sorts of good things. But here's the punchline! The result of all that would be that this great nation from Abraham would bless *all the other families of the earth!*"[30]

"And?" said Mishael, frowning.

"So, that means God has made it *our* job to bless all those families of the earth. Treat them nicely, trade with them fairly, and well, give them an opportunity to choose God also."

"Really?"

And while Phinehas breathed a sigh of deep emotional satisfaction, Betsalel beamed his broadest smile.

"Look, this discussion today has been a bit challenging, to say the least," admitted Oholiab. "It's made me very uncomfortable, and that's an understatement. I'm giving someone, anyone, a challenge to come back next Sabbath and share a family story. I promise I'll tell mine. And I promise I won't get cross!" He looked sheepishly at Betsalel. "My good friend here knows I can get cranky, but I'm always willing to admit when I'm wrong." Betsalel nodded affirmatively, and leaned across to give his old friend an affectionate thump on the back.

"It's a deal, man," grinned Obadiah.

But the following week, when Oholiab settled himself comfortably and asked who had taken his challenge, all eyes looked earthwards. "Like that, is it?" he smiled in a self-satisfied way. "Well, I'll begin and let's see who has the courage to follow me." He began thus:[31]

"There was once an extremely poor, but very loving family who lived on the banks of the Tigris river, not far from its origin, when it is still clean and sweet and fast-flowing. Both parents worked desperately hard, but

30. Gen 12:3

31. Although imaginative, this story utilizes Bible facts. The main details are found in Gen 29:15–30:8; 33:1–3; 35:8.

there was never enough to eat. One day, before she had even become a woman, the eldest girl came to her father, and asked if she could become a slave to earn money for the family. The father refused, but she persisted, and finally a year later he sold her to a sheep-trader in the vicinity, someone he believed was rich enough to treat her well. The ten pieces of silver the family received was a huge help to their finances (although of course, being a mere girl, she could not get the twenty pieces of silver a young man would fetch[32]), but there were many tears when she left. She was given to the sheep-trader's daughter, an extremely beautiful but rather petulant young woman who never even bothered to find out the name of her slave-girl, but merely called her after the town she came from.[33] One day a very handsome young man arrived, apparently a relative of the family, but you can recognize what type of people this girl's masters were by the way they treated this lad. He'd fallen head over heels in love with the slave girl's mistress, and asked to marry her. But the father, the meanest man that side of the Arabian Desert, only agreed to the marriage if the lad worked for him for seven years! I mean, that was a preposterous amount of time, an unthinkable demand! But worse was to follow. At the end of the prescribed time this beast of a man disguised his plain, simpering, elder daughter for whom he'd been unable to find a prospective husband, and palmed her off in disguise as the younger sister! After the nuptial night, it was too late for the young fellow to back out. I mean, he'd already slept with her, which meant no one else would even consider having her. So, his only option was to work another seven years for the girl he loved. Well he did that, unbelievably, and so young Bilhah, as she was known, became part of the bridal dowry. Sadly, her mistress might have been handsome, but she was not fertile, and after droopy-eyed big sister[34] had four kids and she had none, she persuaded her doting husband to take her Bilhah as a concubine, which he did. He only had two encounters with Bilhah, but both produced very healthy, happy boys. Sadly, Bilhah was not allowed to be recognized as their mother, but they had to call her young vixen mistress 'mother', that is, until she finally had a child of her own (who became their father's favorite),[35] and then she had no more time for either of these boys. Actually, that was the best day

---

32. Gen 37:28

33. Bilhah is the name of a town, and seems to have no other special meaning. See Strong's concordance # 1090.

34. Gen 29:17

35. Gen 37:2–3

of their lives. They could finally stop pretending, and be their real mother's sons.

"Well, eventually the young lovesick man had more than he could take of his father-in-law, not really surprisingly. And so too had the old skin-flint's two daughters.[36] They agreed to escape with him, back across the Arabian Desert to his own family. I mean, those women must have been desperate to agree to leave home and journey that far into the unknown! Then out came the reason the young fellow had gone east in the first place — he'd had a big fight with his older brother, whom he'd spectacularly cheated out of the family birthright fortune. He who cheats gets cheated. The guy was terrified by his brother, and when the caravan got near where he lived, in order to protect his own selfish skin, he collected up the two hapless families of his wives' serving women and sent them ahead over the Brook Jabbok so they would encounter the hostile brother first, that is, if he was as hostile as they believed. I mean, talk about courage and chivalry! What a gutless wonder! But amazingly, it seems God was working overtime for this whole miserable family. Not only did spineless Jacob (yes, you guessed right!) have an encounter with God beside the Jabbok Brook, and was never the same afterwards,[37] but his brother had something similar, and was no longer on the war path. So the brothers made up, and all was well.

"Now I come to the good part of the story. That mean sheep trader who would cheat anyone, even his own nephew, once had a sister called Rebekah who really loved her son Jacob, and she was the one who instigated the big cheat operation with the older brother.[38] Seems that family specialized in cheating! Well, she too had a maid. When this maid heard that her mistress's favorite son was coming home she went off to meet him, because her mistress, his mother, had died. There was a very happy reunion. But that dear old lady, who simply said her name was "Busy as a Bee", took the two unfortunate serving wives under her care. She'd had no children of her own, her mistress Rebekah being fertile, and her master Isaac being decent. But she was full of love, love for God and love for any human that crossed her path. She transformed life for my great-great whatever grandmother. Incredibly, when this wonderful old woman, called Deborah,[39] died she was buried with great pomp and ceremony under a terebinth tree and the site

---

36. Gen 31:14–16
37. Genesis chapter 32
38. See Gen 27:1–46
39. Deborah means bee in Hebrew.

honored with the name "Terebinth of Weeping."[40] And so I tell you, because of her the tribes of Asher, Naphtali, and Dan, and I believe Gad also, truly became part of Israel."

As Oholiab finished his story there was some surreptitious wiping of eyes and clearing of throats, but no one spoke.

Finally Phinehas blew his nose vigorously, and said, "I guess you really can say none of us have much to boast about, and but for God we're no better than anyone else."

"Thank you very much Oholiab," said Betsalel, clearing his throat, "for reminding us of the importance of women in our family story. When I think of all the women you mentioned, and then Jochebed and Miriam,[41] the two midwives, Puah and Shiphrah,[42] and of course the Princess Hatshepsut,[43] I have to say that women have done as much for our people as any man has!"

Jahath laughed, awkwardly. "I was going to be brave enough to tell you about my family, about Judah and Tamar and all that sordid mess.[44] But I don't think it's necessary after Oholiab's masterpiece." He paused, then added, "Yes, the real hero, or should I say heroine, in my story is the prostitute Tamar. She was the one who brought Judah to his senses, and made him think so hard that he began his walk with God."

"Don't worry, friend," piped up Joel. "I was going to tell you about my blue-blooded unwantedness! I mean, I come in a direct line from a cheat as a patriarch, and an unwanted woman as a matriarch. Now, who can better that one!" Much laughter followed his remark.

"Don't ask me what my tribe did to our matriarch," said Abitub grinning, but frowning at the same time. "But I think you all know that Rachel, the petulant young woman of Oholiab's story, died giving birth to Benjamin."[45]

"I remember Moses telling me once," said Betsalel quietly, "that God did not choose us because we were better or more numerous or anything superior to other nations, but simply because he loves us."[46]

---

40. Gen. 35:8

41. Exod. 6:20, 15:20

42. Exod. 1:15–21

43. Hatshepsut is widely believed to be the "daughter of Pharaoh" who rescued Moses and later became a Pharaoh in her own right.

44. See Genesis chapter 38.

45. Gen 35:16–20

46. Deut 7:6–11

"You know," said Mikael very softly, "I've finally worked something out. All this time I've been wondering why God hated Egyptians so much. I had a good friend who died in that last plague they had, and that made me very sad, and very angry with God. But now I know God was trying to talk to them. He sent Joseph to save not only us, but also them from that terrible famine that lasted seven years. He put us right in the middle of them so they had every chance learn about our true God. None of them had to die. God was trying to talk with them. And I've finally realized God does not hate Egyptians any more than he hates those traders and E'n'Ms, and the sons of slaves like me and Oholiab. The big issue is whether we choose him or not."

"Exactly," agreed Betsalel. "Perhaps we all need to remember what happened to Moses and his wife Zipporah.[47] She is the sweetest and most gentle woman, but she's a Midianite, not an Israelite. When Aaron and Miriam complained about her, God would not tolerate it, and Miriam was struck with leprosy. She had to be banished out of the camp for a whole week."[48]

"We better start treating each other nicely!" laughed Chelubai.

"And be nice to those traders that come to the camp!" added Mishael. "I've always been too scared to talk to them."

"This is incredible," mused Phineas. "I've been thinking ever since we left Egypt that those Egyptians were hated by God. I mean, all those awful plagues sure looked as though he did! And now it seems God loves everyone, and the big issue is whether or not we choose to love him and are willing to do what he asks."

"The Egyptians aren't the only ones who had plagues," declared Assir stoutly, although his voice trembled a little. "Remember what happened to my family! God loved them, because Betsalel has told us many times that Moses pleaded with them not to rebel. I pleaded with my father. But he and his friends would not listen."

"Aren't we all — I mean everyone in the whole world — from that first pair, Adam and Eve, who rebelled?" asked Joel innocently. "Or, if you prefer, that guy Noah and his three kids."[49]

"The clincher!" exclaimed Obadiah. "None of us has anything to boast about!"

47. Zipporah means small bird, suggesting a pleasant character.

48. See Num. chapter 12.

49. Gen 10: 1–32

6

Encounters with God

As Betsalel went about his work assisting people with broken equipment, or those who needed new tools and materials, he was impressed with the increasing vibrancy amongst the people, and the pervading sense of peace. There had been years of undercurrent grumbling after the terrible rebellions at Kadesh Barnea, but as supporters of the rebels died the mood in the camp daily became more cheerful. Moses had spent much time talking to people, helping them see the mercy and goodness of Yahweh, but it became clear that God was quietly allowing dissenters to die and doing the pacifying work for Moses. Betsalel marveled at how much suffering a few grumblers had caused.

The people were busy, and industry in the camp was generating a significant amount of wealth. No one disagreed with the assertion that they lacked nothing.[1] None of the young men who enjoyed meeting with Betsalel and discussing the issues of life were idle. Two, Chelubai and Jahath, asked Betsalel to teach them his skills, which he was very pleased to do. A deep bond of friendship developed between him and these young men, and although his own tribesmen, they were not the ones he expected might want to work with him.

Kenaz, Obadiah, and Joel were keen herdsmen, but since Joel also loved climbing trees, he encouraged his friends to collect the tiny nuts of the terebinths that grew plentifully around them. They did a steady trade in these nuts with passing merchants. The nuts were used to extract turpentine oils used for healing balsams, but also ground into a bread-making flour.

1. Deut. 2:7

At first Betsalel was puzzled that Phinehas, Assir, and Mishael developed a sandal-making business. Then he realized Phinehas had a steady supply of animal skins from his father, the priest Eleazar, as the hides from burnt offerings belonged to the priests.[2] Involving his Levite cousins in work that made durable rawhide sandals that were quickly traded was a great idea. Whilst the raw oxhide was great for the soles of the sandals, the young men soon learned it was not good for the ties, and they began simple tanning to make soft leather. Because the initial cleaning of the raw skins before tanning was smelly and dirty, Moses allowed them to work only at the edge of the encampment, where they could dam pools of water from the river from the rock, and utilize excrement from the middens to treat the leather. Once the leather was clean it was tanned by the readily available supply of acacia wood bark. Although the Israelite shoes did not wear out, there was a steady demand for these sandals from passing Ishmaelite traders.

Oholiab was a skilled repair workman, but he was also interested in cooking, no doubt influenced by his Naphtali and Asher tribal neighbors who were renowned for their fine cuisine.[3] He soon persuaded Mikael help him make delicious sweet treats much in demand by the women in the camp.

Abitub and his brother Elpaal joined their mother in her weaving business, and were very successful. They often spoke of the fun they had making patterns with natural wool colors, and especially with dyeing. They admitted dyeing was a very expensive activity, and they could not afford to fool around with the precious indigo and purple pigments, but they never ceased enjoying the work.

All the boys, rapidly becoming young men, retained their interest in birds, so there was much excitement when Joel and Kenaz discovered a large eagle foraging in a midden at the edge of the camp.

"It's wings must have been at least five cubits!" Joel excitedly reported to the others in the group.

"And you should have seen its legs" added Kenaz. "That birds wears breeches!" They proudly led the group out to the midden, and to their joy the bird was still there.

2. Lev 7:8

3. Gen 49:20–21

"Wow!" exclaimed Phinehas, the bird authority. "I've never seen that before! But I've heard about them, and I think it's a steppe eagle, a migratory bird."[4]

Thus, with life settling into a placid routine, Betsalel finally felt ready to keep the promise he had made his young friends. But he decided to make it a surprise.

As his friends entered his tent for their next gathering, one by one they were struck mute by the sight of Moses sitting cross-legged on a large cushion. Clearly, Moses was enjoying the joke because he said nothing until all were assembled, then smilingly announced, "Now let's see if I can recognize you all." Joel was about to declare that there was no way he could recognize any of them, but awe fortunately kept his mouth shut. None noticed the triumphantly beaming face of Betsalel behind the gentle leader.

"Now," began Moses, pointing determinedly, "I certainly know you Phinehas, and Assir and Mishael. All of you are in your apprenticeships for priesthood and Levite duties, aren't you?"[5] The three young men nodded in awed silence.

"Now, I need to apologize to you all for taking so long to come and join you. Betsalel has repeatedly asked me, but sorting out the complaints and concerns of people is a time consuming business. The good news is most people in the camp are now content and not causing trouble. But we have to keep vigilant and uphold the glory of Yahweh all the time."

This unexpected apology surprised everyone, and Joel blurted out, "Don't worry! We're just very pleased to see you!"

"Ah yes, you're Joel from Issachar, aren't you?" Joel gasped in astonishment. "And there are the Benjamin boys, Abitub and Elpaal! How's your mother's weaving business progressing? Now, no Judahite should be hiding his face from me, and I see Kenaz, Jahath and Chelubai, if I'm not mistaken, right? And who else have we here? Ah, yes, Obadiah from Zebulun, and Mikael from Gad, and of course my very good, very old friends, Oholiab and Betsalel!" Moses paused, and then added, "Ah yes, these are the names[6] — that's how I've begun my second book." After another pause Moses

4. Steppe eagles are indeed migratory, and pass from wintering grounds in Africa through the Middle East to their breeding grounds in Russia, Kazakhstan, Mongolia, and China.

5. Numb 4:47 indicates that the Levites served from ages 30 to 50, but Numb 8:23–25 says the ages for service were 25 to 50. This suggests there was a five-year apprenticeship, understandable because the sanctuary regulations were complex.

6. Exod. 1.1

observed, "You have a fine group, but you need to include people from Reuben, Simeon, Naphtali and Asher."

"Don't worry," smiled Oholiab, "I'm working on Naphtali and Asher, and Mikael is doing his best to get some Reubenites and Simeonites to join our chat group."

Suddenly Moses shocked them, throwing back his head and bursting into a deep rollicking laugh. "I fooled you all, didn't I?" he said, chuckling merrily. "Do you really think I know the names of everyone in the camp?"

Now Betsalel laughed. "But I can tell you, Moses does have a very good memory. Before you arrived he asked me to give him a description of you all, and your names, and you have to admit he made good use of it!"

Kenaz gasped. "So you're human after all!"

Moses nodded. "Exactly. Now you won't be scared of me, promise?"

"Betsalel said you would tell us about the bush," spoke up Jahath. "I've been wanting to know about that for years. And could you please explain about circumcision. It seems a pretty gruesome business to me, and I can't see what purpose it has."

"Yes I will tell you about the bush, and I'm delighted you're interested. But first, let's talk about circumcision. Circumcision is the sign of the renewed covenant God made with Abraham. The first covenant God made with Abraham was sealed with the blood of a heifer, a she-goat, a ram, a turtle dove, and a pigeon.[7] But when he could not have a child with Sarah Abraham didn't trust God, and took Hagar as his wife.[8] So, after this God renewed the covenant, and this time it was sealed with Abraham's own blood, by circumcision."[9]

"But that's weird!" exclaimed Kenaz. "It's just plain barbaric!"

Moses continued, apparently ignoring Kenaz. "Yahweh never explained why he chose circumcision. Maybe it's because it involves the organ Abraham used to sin. Maybe it's close to the heart or center of a man. After Abraham's circumcision God tried to make it easier, and so Isaac was circumcised when he was just eight days old.[10] A baby that old will have minimal pain and certainly won't remember it. All of you were circumcised as babies in Egypt, weren't you, and how many of you remember anything

7. Gen 15:9–21
8. Gen 16:1–16
9. Gen 17:4–11
10. Gen 17:12–14, 21:4

about it? But circumcision is meant to show that we are seriously chosen as God's people."

There was much murmuring among the boys, who obviously still did not understand. "I guess he's right," muttered Mishael. "It was pretty painless for us, not such a big deal. But it must have been horrible for Abraham, who was ninety-nine years old!"[11]

"My parents forgot, so I was about eight years old when I was circumcised. It was horrible! That's why I've been so keen to know what circumcision is all about. I'm sure Abraham never forgot! It must have been excruciating for him!" exclaimed Jahath. "But I'm beginning to understand that maybe it isn't so barbaric after all." He was silent for a while, and then grinned. "I hope you won't think I am very bad, Moses, but do you think God has a bit of a sense of humor about this circumcision business? I mean, it seems such a big deal to us, and you've all heard me call it barbaric. But when we're walking around no one knows whether we're circumcised or not! It seems it's meant to be a secret pact between God and the man!"

Moses nodded thoughtfully. "Son, I think you're on to something. Yahweh always has a reason for what he asks of us. Maybe God likes to mark his people so that they can always, permanently, know they belong to him. Yes, but maybe it is a bit more of a secret, between just the man and God. Hadn't thought of that, but it's a nice idea. We aren't meant to parade our own goodness to others, but to live lives that show we belong to Yahweh."

"I was talking to some young kids who were born out here in the desert, and I discovered they hadn't been circumcised yet," Assir remarked, obviously concerned.

"That's right," said Moses. "Yahweh will reveal the right time for them to be circumcised. It's not your concern. Circumcision means total commitment to God, and it shouldn't be just a ritual. Yes, Yahweh will show when it is time for these desert-born people to be circumcised."[12]

Much discussion followed this. All the boys liked the idea that it was a secret pact between God and the man concerned, although some still expressed concern that it was such a painful ordeal. Betsalel suggested that it was a good way of teaching that sin is a distressing business — its results always hurt someone.

11. Gen 17:10–14, 22–27

12. Josh. 5:2–9. Why no one was circumcised during the desert wanderings is not explained, but we are told they were circumcised before the conquest of Canaan.

Finally Phinehas dared ask, "Now, please, tell us about the burning bush Moses."

"I will. But would you like me to tell you about my life before that?"

"How much can you remember?" asked Mikael with a grin. "Even the ark in the papyrus?"

Moses chuckled. "I'm glad you know that part of my story, but I confess I don't remember it! I was simply going to tell you how I spent forty years in this wilderness, and nearly ended my days here. My mother Jochebed[13] was a wonderful woman, as were both my parents. She only had charge of me for a few years, but she made sure I knew where I came from."

"I remember her," butted in Assir, while Phinehas and Mishael nodded. "She told amazing stories about the ancestors."

"She did," said Moses. "She inspired me with the idea that Yahweh would use me to rescue Israel from the Egyptians, so when I went to the palace I started planning just that, right from the time I got there, even though I was very young. The Princess Hatshepsut, later Pharaoh,[14] was extremely good to me, and protected me from the angry, officious priests who were enraged that I would not join in their religious rites. When those priests gained the upper hand and assassinated her, I was in a very awkward situation. But, instead of relying on the El Shaddai of my Fathers, I decided my own ability and military training was sufficient to deal with the situation, and the time to start the liberation of Israel had arrived. May I plead with you to never forget that it is never, ever, right to run ahead of God! Trust Yahweh, and wait for him is my urgent advice. Giving God a helping hand is always disastrous. Remember Abraham and Hagar."

"We were talking about the problems that resulted from Abraham's running ahead of God last time we gathered," agreed Chelubai. "I confess I can see trouble for many, many years to come!"

"Yes, sadly Abraham's mistake did, and will, cause trouble, lots of it. Everyone knows I killed the taskmaster, was discovered, and had to flee for my life. Now I'm deeply ashamed about what I did, but God was merciful to me, and directed me to Midian, a country I knew little about. I

13. Exod. 6:20

14. Whilst there is some difference of opinion, the most reasonable date for the Exodus is approximately 1450 BC, thus Hatshepsut would have been the Pharaoh's daughter at the time of Moses' birth, and she became Pharaoh during 22 years of his time in the palace. About the time of his flight to Midian a coup removed Hatshepsut, and endangered Moses' position, but his own action provided the final trigger. This information is from multiple sources, see Bibliography.

think some of you met one of my friends from there?" Moses smiled and looked at Abitub and Elpaal, who nodded eagerly. "Yes, there are many fine Midianites, like my friend, and like my father-in-law Reul. (And by the way, his name means 'friend of God', and his other name, Jethro, means excellence, which was what the people called him because he was such a good man. My wife's name, Zipporah, means 'bird'.) They worship the same God as we do, El Shaddai, and as I talked with Reul gaps in my mother's stories were filled in. I discovered that Midianites were descendants of Abraham, just like I was."

"Oh, wow, more of them!" exclaimed Obadiah.

"Yes, their matriarch was called Keturah,[15] whom Abraham married after Sarah died. I had a lot of time to think out there in the desert with the sheep, and I began jotting notes, comparing my mother's stories with Jethro's, and was astonished at the way they matched. God had certainly led me to the right man to gain understanding about the story of my people, although I could not see how any of this could ever help me regain opportunity to free them. I simply gave up the idea, and tried to discover the goodness of God's leading in other people's lives. I wrote this in the book called *Beginnings*.[16] Jethro told me about a man called Job, who had many terrible tragedies, but remained true to God, and was eventually greatly honored and rewarded.[17]

"Well, one summer, a dry one when fodder was scarce, I took the flock much further west than usual. I knew I was far from home, and this reminded me of my own weakness and need of protection. I spent much time pleading with El Shaddai to forgive me for making such a mess of my opportunities in Egypt, and begging him to raise up someone to help my people. One morning I was horrified to see a bush burning, and realized in the hot and dry climate of the desert both I and my flock were in great danger. The flock, however, were nonchalantly chewing grass quite a distance away, and seemed unconcerned and safe enough, so I went to look at the fire and see what I could do about putting it out," Moses paused, and gazed into the distance.

15. Gen 25:1–6

16. The Hebrew name for Genesis means Beginning. Many scholars believe Genesis may have been written while Moses was in Midian.

17. See Job chapters 1—2 and 42. Job came from the land of Uz which is believed to be in the vicinity of Midian. Uz was a descendant of Esau, see Gen 36:28. That Job was known to Reul is conjecture, but reasonable supposition. Several scholars consider Job was written during Moses' time in Midian.

Desert Encounter.

"Ah," he continued, "that fire was mesmerizing, magnetic, glorious, amazing.[18] I was utterly spellbound! As I got closer I could see the bush was radiant with flames, but the branches and leaves continued bright green! Incredible! I went closer, and then a voice said to me, 'Moses! Moses!' What a shock! Not only did the bush burn but it talked! I said, 'Here I am', feeling really stupid talking to a bush, and then, oh then!"[19]

Moses stopped, and his face glowed with radiant joy as he looked heavenwards.[20] "Lads," he said softly, as he lowered his gaze, "I don't know how or when God will call you, but it's the most wonderful, and terrifying, thing. But answer that call, please. God told me to come no closer to the bush, and to take my shoes off because I was standing on holy ground. I've never moved so fast! God told me he knew all about the suffering of Israel, and he planned their deliverance and would bring them to the land promised our Fathers. Then he shocked me. I, me, Moses, the man who had messed up by slaying the Egyptian, was still the person he wanted to send to Pharaoh to get release of our people!"[21]

Moses stopped, and his eyes filled with tears. "I refused, yes, I refused. Can you believe it, I refused God! And I had good reasons! Five times there in the desert I told God I couldn't do the job, and after I actually got to Egypt and I had that disastrous first encounter with Pharaoh and he made everyone work without straw, I offered God another two very good reasons why he should find someone else.[22] Can you believe it, seven times I tried to say no to Yahweh! I marvel at how patient God was with me! You know, most people in this camp were awed by the Egyptian plagues, the crossing of the Red Sea, and I agree they were stupendous events. I will never deny that. But imagine the Great God of heaven, the Creator of everything, the Redeemer of Israel, stooping to patiently argue with a mere frightened shepherd in the wilderness!"

Again Moses paused, his face was suffused with radiance. Then he smiled. "Well, I said no seven times, and Yahweh told me seven times what he would do. One of my complaints, believe it or not, was that the people would not know which god I was talking about. I know you'll think that was crazy, but the trouble was I'd spent too much time with those Egyptians

18. In his written account of his call, Moses mentioned fire many times, Exod. 3:2–3

19. See Exod. 3:1–10.

20. Compare Exod. 34:29–35

21. Exod. 3:7–10

22. Exod. 3:11, 13, 4:1, 10, 13, 5:22–23, 6:12.

priests and all their incredible multitude of deities. Of course Israel has only ever had one God, but God patiently explained this to me. He gave himself a special new name, saying, 'Say this to the people of Israel, *I am who I am*, or I will be who I will be, or even *I was who I was*, that is, who has sent you.'[23] Later, when I made my last efforts to get out of the job of leadership, God told me he was called El Shaddai by Abraham, Isaac and Jacob (the same name my father-in-law Reul used) , but now he wanted to be known by this special name, Yahweh,[24] which is a short form of that strange 'I am who I am.' El, or Elohim, is of course the basic name for our mighty God. Now as you know, the word *shad* is Hebrew for breast, so El Shaddai means the mighty God who supplies everything, who is our provider and also protector. But this precious new name Yahweh indicates God is the Living God, the one near us, beside us, with us, the one who is merciful to us, the one who is always with us. I'm so ashamed that I did not immediately appreciate what Yahweh was telling me. I was so busy thinking about a mere name, that I completely missed the important idea that God was telling me he would be right beside me whenever I went to the formidable Pharaoh. Oh how blind we mere mortals are! And can you believe it, I still kept on making excuses to God, telling him I couldn't do the job! I had so many excuses: the people wouldn't listen to me, that I was no good at speaking, and just plain please send someone else! You know, God even got angry with me, but he did not destroy me.[25]

"Yes, Yahweh knew all about me. He knew where I came from, how my patriarch Levi had been cruel and murderous,[26] just as I had been to that Egyptian slave taskmaster, but he still chose to use me. When I made my final excuses to God he came through with his final incredible promises. God spoke to me and said, 'I am Yahweh. I appeared to Abraham to Isaac and to Jacob as El Shaddai. I established my covenant with them to give them the land of Canaan. I have heard their groanings and I have remembered my covenant. Say therefore to the people, I am Yahweh. *I will* bring you from under the burdens of the Egyptians. *I will* deliver you from slavery. *I will* redeem you with an outstretched arm. *I will* take you to be my

23. Exod. 3:13–15

24. No one knows how this should be spoken. To avoid taking God's name in vain Hebrew people substituted Adonai, meaning Lord, instead of saying the written name. It may have been pronounced as Yahveh, but certainly not Jehovah which is an unfortunate misunderstanding of Hebrew.

25. Exod. 4:14

26. Gen 34:25–31

people. *I will* be your God. I am Yahweh your God. *I will* bring you to the land I promised. *I will* give it to you to possess. I am Yahweh.[27]

"Now, did you hear it, brothers, did you hear it? Did you *really* hear it?" Moses almost shouted in his excitement, then added softly. "Seven times I told God I couldn't, and seven times he told me he could, that he will! When I finally realized the truth of what God had said I could face Pharaoh." Moses lifted his radiant face heavenward once again, closed his eyes and clasped his hands in an attitude of supplication.

No one moved. No one spoke. Finally, one by one, all bowed their heads and prayed with Moses.

When Moses opened his eyes he chuckled, right in the middle of his prayer! "I must tell you about the snakes," he smiled. "Yahweh really does have a sense of humor! Now God had given me this snake sign out in the desert: when I threw my rod on the ground it became a *nachash*, an ordinary serpent. Of course I was scared, but I picked it up by the tail as ordered by God and it became my rod again. Well, the second time I went to Pharaoh I was told to use this sign to impress him that Yahweh was commanding him to let the Israelites go. You all know Egyptians love snakes, and Pharaoh has a snake on his crown. But when I threw my rod on the ground it did not become an ordinary *nachash*, it became a *tannin*, a sea monster, a crocodile-like thing! Imagine my shock! Poor Aaron was terrified! I tell you it was very impressive, and I began to laugh. But those magicians just smiled, and with their magic turned their own rods into monsters. I was starting to feel very silly, when suddenly my nasty toothy croc creature slithered over to theirs, and gobbled them all up! It was very funny, but Pharaoh was not amused."[28] Moses stopped smiling, and bowed his head once again and worshipped.

When, after a long time, Moses opened his eyes and saw the youth around him praying, his face again glowed with a holy radiance. One by one they opened their eyes, and smiled at him. When the last person had opened their eyes, Moses spoke, very softly.

"You know, I'm not the only person God has called. God always calls more than one person. He did not just send me to rescue Israel, but also sent my brother Aaron, and the first thing we were to do was to talk to

---

27. Exod. 6:2–8

28. Exod. 4:2–5, 7:8–13. English translations do not accurately indicate that in front of Pharaoh the rod did not become a simple snake, but rather a dragon, a sea monster.

the elders.[29] Two of you, sitting right here before me, have been called by name, and all of you have been called by covenant. When I was on the mountain for those amazing forty days, God spoke to me seven times. He gave me instructions for building the sanctuary. The sixth time he came and talked to me, he told me he had called Betsalel and Oholiab to be his special workmen.[30] Next time I come maybe we should talk about that."

"What did he say on the seventh time?" whispered Betsalel.

"He told me about the Sabbath, again," smiled Moses. "But you know, the reason those terrible plagues fell was not because Yahweh hated Egyptians, but because he wanted them to learn about him, to recognize their own gods were useless, and to acknowledge his goodness and greatness, to worship him. It's so sad, but they would not listen. They just absolutely refused, or most of them did."[31]

"Uncle Moses," said Mishael. "I just thought of something. I remember God made the world in seven days, right? The last day was about the Sabbath, and the sixth day was about people. Does the sanctuary have anything to do with God's creation? I mean the last speech he gave you was about the Sabbath, and if the sixth was about Betsalel and Oholiab, they were people. Is there some connection between creation and the sanctuary?"

"That's a wonderful observation," agreed Moses. "The seven days of creation clearly show us we belong to God because he made us. The sanctuary and it services are to show us how Yahweh plans to restore and remake our world by dealing with and finally getting rid of sin. I'd like to talk to you more about this, if we can work out a suitable time."

"That's encouraging," observed Mikael. "God always does things in such an orderly, precise way. It sure seems he has everything under control. And yes, it would be great to talk more!"

Moses nodded, and was silent as he pondered Mishael's and Mikael's comments. The boys wriggled and moved their cramped limbs. Joel raised his hand.

"What is it, son?" asked Moses.

"I just wanted to say thank you so much for talking to us," said Joel breathlessly. "I do hope you really will come again!"

"Of course," agreed Moses.

29. Exod. 4:29–31
30. Note Exod. 25:1, 30:11, 17, 22, 34, 31:1, 12.
31. Exod. 7:5, 17, 22 etc.

"One thing," asked Mikael, "did Betsalel refuse God seven times like you did?"

"No son," said Moses, a broad smile illuminating his face, "he didn't!"

7

Becoming One

Joel was running so fast he almost collided with Betsalel. He stopped short, panting heavily, and Betsalel looked up from the cheese vat he was mending for the wife of Gameliel, leader of the tribe of Manasseh.[1]

"What's up?" asked Betsalel, somewhat alarmed. "Something wrong?"

"I just," began Joel, still breathing heavily, "I just came to tell you" — more heavy breathing — "the news. Phineas is getting married!"

"About time!" responded Betsalel, smiling broadly. "But I thought everyone knew."

"He's marrying Chelubai's sister. Did you know that?" Clearly Joel was a little disappointed that he was not bringing Betsalel unexpected news.

"Well, you must remember that Chelubai and I work together. So I heard the whispers of Phineas and his interest in Maryam."

Joel squatted down beside Betsalel and watched him working. "Yeah, I forgot that Chelubai works with you. Of course you'd know."

Betsalel continued his hammering. Then he looked up, his eyes twinkling mischievously.

"Since you've run right across camp to tell me this great news, I think I should reward you with some more news. Who else do you think might be getting married?"

Joel looked up sharply. "Someone else? This is getting like a disease!"

Betsalel threw back his head and laughed heartily. "Wait till it's your turn! I don't think you'll have any trouble getting some beautiful young woman to agree to spend her life with you!"

---

1. Numb 2:20.

Joel blushed brilliantly. "Father says I have to wait," he said sheepishly.

"But not too long, I'll vouch for that," smiled Betsalel. "Your dad had a chat with me! Would her name be Milcah, by any chance?"

"Did he really?" exclaimed Joel. "When Father talked to me it sounded as though he'd never give consent!"

"Then cheer up," grinned Betsalel. "By the way he was talking to me he seems very happy with your young lady. He just wants to make sure you are serious about her, and that it's not just a passing fancy."

"Passing fancy!" exploded Joel. "About Milcah,[2] the most wonderful girl in the whole camp! Dad must be crazy!"

"I think all parents want to make sure their children have chosen wisely and well. So just keep on acting wisely and well yourself, and in no time you and Milcah will be starting a new life together."

A gentle silence fell, broken only by the scraping of Joel's stick as he scratched pictures in the dust. "You know," he finally said. "You've just given me the best news yet. I thought I was racing over here to give you a bit of exciting information, and it turns out it's you who's brought great joy and encouragement to me. I honestly thought Father would never consent for us to get married, but now that I think about it, he always had a very cheerful smile when he talked to me. You know, I was so scared, I always thought that smile was about how young and silly I was. But really he was just testing me, right?"

"Exactly," said Betsalel, standing up, and admiring his handiwork. "Rushing into marriage is always very foolish. Just be thankful you have good and caring parents."

"I guess you're right."

Gamaliel's wife came over and began thanking Betsalel for his help. They chatted in a friendly way, and she asked how much of her cheese he would accept as payment for his labor. Joel noticed Betsalel's charges were extremely fair, and once again had a surge of pride and gratitude for his friendship with the man who had so much enriched his life. Finally the good woman moved away.

When she was out of earshot, Joel said quietly, "She's a great woman. The sort of woman I'd like to have! I'm sure Milcah is just like her."

"She is," agreed Betsalel.

2. Representative name, see Num 36:10–11.

"But Betsalel, I discovered you know my news, and we've talked about my little secret. But you said someone else is getting married. Now who is that?"

"There's going to be a double wedding. When Phineas and Maryam get married, so is Chelubai."

"Chelubai!"

"Surprised?" Chuckling, Betsalel began collecting his tools.

"I guess we shouldn't really be surprised about Phineas getting married," observed Joel. "After all, he was the eldest of our group, right?"

"Yes, he was. And you were always such a warm-hearted young fellow that I'm not surprised that you've found someone you love."

"But Chelubai, now that *is* a surprise," repeated Joel.

"Look, just because he's a steady, quiet, young man doesn't mean he doesn't have eyes and feelings," grinned Betsalel.

"True," mused Joel. Then turning full to Betsalel, and grabbing his friend by the shoulder, he added, "I've got it! The bride price their family gets for Maryam they can give to Chelubai's girl's family! All so clean and sweet!"

"I didn't think you were so mercenary minded!" laughed Betsalel. "Are you thinking of such an idea for your Milcah?"

"Of course not!" exclaimed Joel, suddenly horrified by his own suggestion.

"Yeah," agreed Betsalel. "I don't think anyone wants to be like that despicable Laban who made poor Jacob work fourteen years for his wives, and turned the whole beauty and joy of marriage into a cheap commercial transaction."[3]

"Yeah, my mother always reminded me that the words for Laban and Egyptian-style brickmaking come from the same root."[4]

"Yes, Moses told me the same thing. He often mentioned the story of the tower. You remember, the one people made of bricks that they thought could reach to heaven? The one called confusion, or Babel."[5]

Joel nodded thoughtfully.

"That tower story tells us exactly how we are *not* meant to work," Betsalel continued. "Those people were so full of themselves, so full of

3. Gen 29:15–30

4. Hebrew is based on "roots" of consonants, usually three. The root *lbn* can mean to whiten, or brickmaking, as well, of course, as being the core of the name Laban.

5. Gen 11:1–9

proud conceit. I guess we all experienced the tower-type way of working in Egypt. It was never about helping people, but all about making someone look wonderful and important! Just money, money, money! But remember the call of Abraham? How God called him out of his culture and told him he should be a blessing to others?[6] I often remind myself of that when I'm doing my work. I don't see my work as a way of getting rich and taking advantage of others, of being important. But I do ask myself if I am blessing others."

"I guess that applies to getting married too, doesn't it?" asked Joel. "I've certainly decided that having more than one wife is most definitely not the way to bring blessing to anything! It sure didn't bring blessing to Abraham and Sarah,[7] and the family of Jacob was extremely miserable, and don't we all know that! No blessing there!"[8]

"You're absolutely right. Moses told me many times that having more than one woman was never God's plan. But we're all slow to learn, and there are lots of families in this camp with multiple wives. But I can tell you those homes are not happy ones. However, God is remarkably patient with us as he tries to help us learn his way."

"Milcah's definitely the only one for me!"

"Yes, I understand. That's why I never remarried," said Betsalel. Joel was about to ask what had happened to Betsalel's wife, but noticing the intense cloud of anguish that passed over his friend's face, decided it was not the time to enquire. He kicked some stones in the path as they walked back to the eastern side of the camp.

Betsalel finally broke the awkward silence between them. "I suppose you'd like to know who Chelubai is marrying?"

Grateful of this new topic, Joel eagerly agreed.

"Her name is Deborah, the same name of the wonderful woman who was such a help to Rebecca, the woman Oholiab told us about when we were struggling to accept each other and all our different backgrounds. Remember?"

"Yes, I do remember that powerful story. If I recall rightly we decided that we all have difficult family stories, with very few things we can be proud of, but much more often things we are deeply ashamed of. So much of our misery came from stupid and miserable marriages, if I understood things properly."

6. Gen 12:1–3
7. Gen 16:4–6; 21:9–14
8. Gen 29:31–35; 30:1–24

Joel's Love.

"Yes, you certainly got that idea right. Anyway, Deborah comes from the tribe of Judah just as Chelubai does, and the plan is that Chelubai and Deborah, and Phineas and Maryam will get married together. Preparations are well underway."

"So, Eleazar will have to kill the fatted calf for them?" laughed Joel.

"That's definitely what happened with other weddings that have cheered our desert wanderings. But it's interesting, both couples have decided to dispense with the calf. Eleazar protested about this, and insisted he wanted to give his son the best, a really good wedding party, but both Phineas and Chelubai had a long talk with him and convinced him it was not necessary."

"Really?" Joel shook his head dubiously.

"Apparently Phineas has nightmare memories of the time when the whole of Israel complained about having to eat manna all the time, and God apparently miraculously provided quails in abundance for the people, but they died of food poisoning even while they were eating."[9]

"I sure remember that!" said Joel, shuddering. "It was so sad. I've always wondered why God didn't send healthy quails so people didn't die."

"Yes, I've had the same thoughts. But the people never asked if the quails were meant for food. They just attacked those poor birds! Many people didn't even bother to cook the meat properly. Anyway, both Phineas and Chelubai decided they don't need flesh for their wedding, and have thought of other special things. Phineas knows when he becomes a fully functional priest he'll have to eat the meat of the offerings, at least some of it to show that he carries the sin of the people, but he says there's no reason why he has to start eating this sooner than he has to![10] There'll be plenty of raisons and pistachios, and lots of the very best cheeses at this wedding. I've heard Eleazar has arranged for some fine Egyptian flour to be available, so there will be various types of special leavened bread. I know Eleazar got special permission from Moses and Aaron to get this flour, as he was not quite sure if it was the right thing to do. Eleazar is always very careful to do the right thing, especially after the death of his brothers. And I know Chelubai's mother has been developing some amazing dishes from manna, and she's even arranged that there will be cucumbers and garlic available! Honestly, I think even the most dedicated adherent to Egyptian cuisine will

9. Numb 11:4–6, 31–35.

10. See for example, Lev 10:16–18

be very impressed with what is being planned for this wedding, but no meat anywhere!"

"Very interesting," responded Joel. "What do the brides have to say about all this? They should have some choice about it, surely!"

"That's what I thought," said Betsalel. "I discovered the young women were more than happy to dispense with meat, both of them being very tender-hearted girls, and not at all interested in killing any animals. I have to admit at first I did think it was odd, and even talked to Moses about it. To my surprise he reminded me that eating meat was never God's initial plan, that originally plants were the diet chosen for humans[11] and that it was only after the Great Flood destroyed everything that humans were given permission to eat meat.[12] I think we've talked about that in the past, right?"

Joel nodded. "You've just about convinced me to also have a meatless wedding celebration. I'll talk to Milcah about it, and see what she thinks. A wedding should really be all about the couple (or couples), shouldn't it? But I have to be honest, this one sounds like it will have a really interesting menu, and I confess I'm starting to look forward to it just for that! By the way, do you know the date for the celebration?"

"Yes, it will be when the moon is full later this month."

"That's a lovely time for a wedding! But there won't be any Egyptian strong drink, will there?" asked Joel, a little anxiously.

"Most definitely not, not after what happened to Eleazar's brothers,"[13] declared Betsalel adamantly.

"That's good to know. I remember that wedding a few months ago over in the Ephraim camp. I don't know how they got it, but I understand beer is pretty easy to make once you have some flour and water and just let it ferment. Afterall, leavened flour makes good bread. Anyway, at that wedding there was plenty of this strong drink, and the behavior of the people was atrocious."

"Yes, it was a very sad occasion. Fortunately the priests and Levities quickly got the situation under control. Now that I think of it, Phineas himself was involved with getting things back to law and order, so I'm doubly sure he will not be having any strong drink for his own wedding!"

11. Gen 1:29

12. Gen 9:1–17

13. See Lev 10:1–11. "Strong drink" was the biblical name for beer (distillation for making spirits being unknown at this time). Wine, of course, was from the juice of grapes, which may or may not have been fermented, and not readily available to people wandering in a desert.

By now the men had reached the eastern side of the encampment, the place of their own tents, and prepared to separate.

"Perhaps we should get all the group together and introduce the new female members of the team," suggested Betsalel with a smile.

"Fantastic idea!" agreed Joel. "I'll talk to Phineas and Chelubai, and ask my father if he thinks it would be appropriate for me to introduce Milcah to the others. What do you think?" Betsalel nodded, and the men parted to go to their tents.

Joel was just about to turn the corner into his own line of tents when Betsalel called him. Turning, he saw Betsalel beckoning. Thinking his friend had more news, he ran back eagerly.

"Sorry to bother you, but I'd like to share something," began Betsalel diffidently.

Joel shrugged and waited for the news, surprised that Betsalel seemed lost for words.

Betsalel coughed, cleared his throat, and laid his hand on Joel's shoulder. "Women are wonderful friends," he began awkwardly, "but they're not like men."

Despite Betsalel's serious manner, Joel could not help laughing. "Isn't that obvious!" he finally managed to say between chortles.

"Well, maybe not too obvious, at least many men don't understand women well. Women are different, sensitive, soft hearted. If you treat a woman just like you treat a man, you'll be in for some nasty shocks."

By now Joel had stopped chuckling, and realized his friend and mentor was trying to share something really important.

"Think of a woman as bringing balance into your life, of helping you see things from a new perspective." There was an awkward pause, and then Betsalel continued. "I'm sharing something it took me a long while to learn, too long, I'm sad to relate. But I'm glad I did learn it before it was too late."

"Thanks for sharing," Joel murmured.

"You know the story of how God made humans," Betsalel continued after a gentle pause. "Moses used to emphasize to me that God said he made humans in 'our' image, meaning that God is one, yet has more than one aspect.[14] I know the Spirit of God was poured into me, an incredible thought.[15] I often wondered what exactly that meant, because I certainly wasn't God, but there was something very different about me after that happened. The

14. Gen 1:26–27
15. Exod. 31:1–11

Spirit of God is God, is Yahweh, the eternally-being God, the God who has always existed, and always will exist, the One Moses told us he saw when he was hidden in the rock on Mount Sinai after the terrible calf rebellion. But the Spirit of God brings another aspect of God into our lives."[16]

"All of that is very mysterious," replied Joel thoughtfully. "I'm not at all sure I understand it."

"You know, I think it's a good thing you don't. I don't. In fact, I think the most dangerous state for anyone to be in is to think they know everything about something."

Joel grinned. "So you suggest that I don't try to think I know everything about Milcah, that she's exactly the same as me and I can do all her thinking for her!"

"Exactly!" exclaimed Betsalel, beaming with delight. "Let her be an exciting and unfolding mystery for you, an enchanting someone who is always a delight to discover more about!"

"I hope she'll find learning about me exciting," mused Joel, very seriously.

"I think she will. But the amazing thing Moses told me was that when people get married God said they become one. Just like Yahweh and the Spirit are one. That's a huge mystery, but it does sound very lovely don't you think? Two completely different humans combining their unique selves in a love agreement, and then becoming something completely new, a new individual called a married couple!"

16. Exod. 33:17—34:9

8

Consecrated

It was hard to BELIEVE, but almost half the years of wandering in the desert had passed. The vision of teaching others, that brought Betsalel a glimmer of hope on the fateful day of the Korah, Dathan, and Abiram rebellion, had never left him. But those boys were now young men, holding serious responsibilities, most married with homes of their own. The marriages had all been joyous affairs. The meatless feast for the double wedding of Phineas and Maryam and Chelubai and Deborah was so successful that Joel and Milcah decided to follow their example. One by one all the other members of the group decided to do the same, and agreed that years of eating manna had given them a new perspective on what was delicious food.

Phinehas and his three cousins, the sons of Ithamar, Aaron's youngest son, were now active priests.[1] There had been an elaborate ceremony that lasted seven days for the dedication the first priests to their office.[2] After the terrible Korah rebellion, God settled the permanent and perpetual priesthood of Aaron and his sons by the symbolic blossoming of Aaron's almond rod.[3] But God also made provision that all new priests should be similarly

---

1. There is no biblical mention of any sons of Ithamar, but it is likely that he did have some.

2. This ceremony was very important and is recorded in command and practice three times, see Exod. 29:1–36; Lev. 8:1–4; Lev. 8:5—9:24.

3. Numb. 17:1—18:4

anointed and consecrated for their God-ordained office.[4] Anointing leaders became a very important rite in Jewish culture.[5]

It was an emotional day for the whole group when they accompanied Phinehas (soon after his marriage) and his cousins to the door of the tabernacle. Joel, in his excitement and awkwardness, caused a moment of serious angst when he quipped, "Phinehas, don't muddle up the fire like Nadab and Abihu did!"[6]

Phinehas turned deadly pale, so pale they thought he was going to faint. Then he smiled wanly, and said steadily, "Don't fear, I won't."

Assir hastily whispered to Joel, "Remember, they were his uncles."

Chelubai put his arm around his sister Maryam, who looked as though she too might faint at the remembrance of what had happened.

"They were scared, terrified," added Mishael softly. "Tried to get Egyptian courage by using beer, but of course that simply destroyed their critical thinking, and that's why they used the wrong fire."[7]

Joel began weeping softly when he realized the inappropriateness of his foolish joke. Betsalel leaned over and squeezed his arm. "Phinehas will understand," he said. Milcah also whispered something to him, and he smiled a weak and watery smile.

"That girl is already good for him," thought Betsalel, delighted their wedding was set for the following month.

Phinehas was wearing his finest *kutōnet* for his consecration, but knew soon his great uncle Moses and grandfather Aaron would strip him of this, ceremonially wash him, and then robe him in the long waist-to-knee breeches and brand new white linen *kutōnet* special for his priestly work, place a special cap on his head, and tie the long sash that was a unique part of priestly robes.[8] The whole service lasted seven days, during which time Phinehas and his cousins could not leave the tabernacle courtyard.[9] Each day a bull and two rams were sacrificed, the bull for a sin offering, one ram

4. Exod.29:29–30

5. Although there is no further record of priests being consecrated, Joshua was "commissioned" by the laying on of hands, see Numb. 27:18–23, Deut. 31: 7–8, 14–15, and kings of Israel were anointed with holy oil, see for example, 1 Sam 10:1 (Saul), 1 Sam 16:13 (David), 2 Chron.23:11 (Joash).

6. Lev. 10:1–11. Whilst not proven, many biblical scholars believe Nadab and Abihu probably died during their ordination, which is recorded in Lev.8:1—9:24.

7. Lev 10:8–11

8. Exod. 28:40–43

9. Lev. 8:33

for a burnt ascension offering, and the other ram for a consecration offering, whose blood was applied to the young men's right ears, right thumbs, and right big toes.[10] However, Phinehas later told his friends that for him the most emotional part of the ceremony was when the anointing oil was poured over him.[11]

"You know," he told Betsalel and Kenaz who were waiting for him when he finally left the courtyard, "it was when that beautiful oil was poured over me that I suddenly felt changed. Wow! I could smell the incredible perfume of holiness on my very self. It was extremely humbling. May I live up to God's plan! Please pray for me."

"We will, never doubt it," assured Kenaz. "I just hope you'll have time to join us sometimes."

"I will, I truly will. But now my duties as a priest must always come first, I'm sure you understand."

Camp life had settled into a gentle routine. Sometimes Betsalel missed his young friends and the regular times they had together. But this was dispelled by a special commission from Moses himself. Moses wanted his people to learn to read and write!

It was well-known that Moses himself could read and write,[12] an accomplishment that inspired awe in the camp. In Egypt, reading and writing was the exclusive achievement of the royal and religious elite. But, of course, Moses had been part of that elite. Elegant hieroglyphs, liberally carved into the walls of virtually all the imposing Egyptian public buildings, were there for all to see, although few could understand the strange signs. Control of information was a tool of the ruling elite. But the most common form of Egyptian writing was hieratic, a simplified cursive form of hieroglyphic not carved into stone, but written in ink with a brush, or stylus, on papyrus sheets. Papyrus reeds grew plentifully along the Nile, the natural sap of the hammered out stems, augmented by waste from tanning, making a good glue for the paper thus produced. Hieratic was used for the numerous legal and commercial documents needed for the successful running of the wealthy Egyptian Empire.[13] Moses would have been very familiar with the complexities of hieratic writing.

---

10. Lev 8:1–29

11. Lev.8:30

12. Exod. 24:4,7

13. https://en.wikipedia.org/wiki/Hieratic 21 July, 2021

No one knows when Moses discovered Phoenician writing,[14] but it was probably while he was in Midian. The Phoenicians, based in Tyre and Sidon, Semitic people like the Israelites, traded widely around the Mediterranean area, and their two languages were no doubt comprehensible to both. Simple Phoenician writing, with only twenty-two characters, (each with their own sound) transformed communication, and Moses was quick to appreciate its worth. At first Moses' writing ability merely gave him an aura of mysticism, because it was believed it took a lifetime of application to learn hieroglyphs. Older people had little interest in obtaining his skills because they could see no value in reading. But as life in the camp settled into a peaceful routine, and his efforts to explain that there was nothing magic about writing, and all that was needed was learning twenty-two signs that could be combined in numerous ways to make an infinity of messages, young people became motivated to learn.[15] Additionally, Moses was writing books that would help his people know their history and the laws of God. That meant it was important that they learn to read.

Phinehas, already strongly interested in the history of his nation, was fascinated to discover during his priestly training that Moses had written several scrolls of intensely valuable history and instructions for his people. Papyrus did not grow in the desert, but what was there in abundance were thousands of sheep whose skins made valuable vellum ready and waiting for ink. Phinehas had already discovered that the skins of burnt ascension offerings became the property of the priests.[16] The more delicate skins of sheep gave them ample material to use for writing, in addition to the less bookishly useful cowhide that Phinehas and his two friends used to make sandals (a business Phineas the priest was happy to pass on to some Levite friends). The priests were only too happy to make these hides available for their Levite cousins to use. Of course the material was much too precious to be used just to practice writing (trays of sand and a stick were a more appropriate option for that), but once the twenty-two characters were mastered, having the opportunity to write not only their own names, but a precious portion of one of Moses' books became a cherished dream of many a young Levite and Israelite.

---

14. https://en.wikipedia.org/wiki/Phoenician_alphabet 21 July, 2021

15. This is conjecture, but the fact remains Jewish people early developed a respect and appreciation for literary skills. This would necessitate they must have been originally taught by someone who had mastered the arts.

16. Lev 7:8

Because Moses, by command of God, had decreed that Levites should take the place of all the firstborn of Israel,[17] they naturally took a leadership role in teaching. For years Betsalel tried to multiply classes such as the one he inaugurated with his twelve young friends, but with apparently little success. But as the idea of reading and writing became popular, suddenly his dream began to come true.

Abitub and Elpaal contacted Eliasaph, head of the Gershonite Levites dwelling with them on the west side of the tabernacle.[18] To their delight he was very enthusiastic about the idea, and soon organized a group of young E'n'Ms, plus Gershonites. As the E'n'Ms discovered the stories of their ancestors they became much friendlier, and ceased teasing their Benjaminite neighbors.

Oholiab gently worked on his younger brother, and convinced him that eating fish was not the most important thing in life. His brother had friends in the tribes of Naphtali and Asher, and soon there were ten of them eagerly sharing ideas from the writings of Moses. The gentle Merarite Levites who camped near them on the north side of the tabernacle were keen to share their reading and writing skills, and their leader Zuriel was most helpful.[19]

For years the long shadow of the rebellion of Korah, Dathan and Abiram had fallen over the Kohathites, the Reubenites, and the Simeonites who lived to the south of the tabernacle. Despite the efforts of Assir and Mishael, not a single Reubenite or Simeonite had ever accepted an invitation to join Betsalel's discussion group. Although they were delighted that Mikael from the tribe of Gad joined the group, he sadly admitted he was often teased by his neighboring tribes for this. Then one day the wife of Elizur, leader of the Reubenites,[20] needed some urgent repairs to her cooking pots. Betsalel was her first resort, and he quickly solved her problems. After the repairs were completed they got talking. Betsalel discovered she was originally from the tribe of Gad, and knew Mikael well.

"He's a fine young man," she observed. "I wish all our tribesmen were as good natured and devout as he is."

Betsalel did not waste his opportunity, and made his usual invitation, without apparent success, until he mentioned these groups included classes

17. Numb. 3:11–51.
18. Numb.3:21–23, 2:18–24.
19. Numb.3:33–36, 2:25–31.
20. Numb.2:10

for reading and studying national history. To his great joy, within days this good woman had gathered a group of eighteen enthusiastic young learners, and best of all their zeal did not lag. Assir and Mishael had no trouble finding neighboring Kohath Levites to help them.[21]

For a while all these burgeoning exploits made Chelubai, Kenaz, and Jahath from Judah, with their good friends Obadiah and Joel, feel rather left out of the action. They were bemoaning their apparent stagnant situation to Betsalel one evening when he suggested, "Why don't you *demonstrate* reading, and how much fun it is."

"What are you talking about?" frowned Jahath, whose love of Betsalel did not stop him asking penetrating questions.

"Doing things differently," smiled Betsalel. "There are lots of kids in this camp now and . . ."

"That merely means lots of oldies have passed on," retorted Jahath.

Betsalel nodded. "Sadly, just as God said," he replied. "Anyway, let's find some of the kids in the neighborhood of our tents and get them to round up their friends. Just call it 'story time' and let's see what happens. By the way, no poaching on the territory of Abitub, or Assir, or Oholiab."

Joel grinned. He still had his youthful exuberance and agreed to give the idea a try. He was sure Milcah would be willing to help with the project, and he was right. Reluctantly the others acquiesced, although clearly they thought it was a madcap plan. The first person Joel encountered was a lively child he thought far too young, but he decided to make his pitch anyway and see what happened.

"Story time?" cried the boy. "Yippee! Wait till I tell my friends." He raced off, then skidded to a halt when Joel shouted after him. "By the way, who are you kid?"

"Abishua," the boy called, running off again. "Son of Phinehas the priest!"[22]

Joel clapped two hands to his forehead. "Praise God!" he exclaimed, in amazement.

Within a couple of days Joel, with the help of Abishua and Milcah, had collected no less than a dozen boys, aged between eight (Abishua) and fourteen, interested in the plan. Chelubai, Kenaz, Jahath and Obadiah were shamed into action, and were delightedly surprised at the positive receptions their lukewarm sales pitches received. Betsalel's idea was very simple.

---

21. Numb. 3:27–31, cf. Numb. 2:10–16.

22. 1 Chron.6:4

Each one of the "old group" would read a favorite passage from the first scroll of Moses, and if there was enough interest Betsalel would tell his own story.

When the appointed evening arrived even Betsalel was astonished to see about fifty eager young faces waiting for the stories. There were even some girls, sisters of those contacted, among the small crowd!

With great ceremony Jahath the doubter unrolled the long scroll Moses had willingly loaned them. There were oohs and aahs, and cries of "What's that?" "Is it magic?" "Is it safe?" Each of the "old gang" was to read his favorite story, which they had taken the trouble to prearrange so there would be no embarrassing doubling up, but they also agreed to a random order in the stories they shared.

"The LORD appeared to Abraham by the terebinths of Mamre," began Jahath, and continued to read the story of God coming to earth to tell Abraham that he and his wife Sarah would have a son, and how they had both laughed at the crazy idea.[23] The youngsters were all laughing as Jahath handed the scroll on to Kenaz, and there were cries of "That baby was Isaac!"

Kenaz took the scroll from Jahath and rolled it back a little. After a tantalizing pause he read, "And the people said to one another, 'Come let us make bricks,'" and then shared the story of how these foolish people made a tower that was supposed to keep them safe, but God muddled their language and it all came to a miserable halt.[24]

As he ended a small voice was clearly heard, "Did they make something like a pyramid?"

"No, silly," he was answered by a rather self-assured young woman. "Didn't you hear the tower was called Babel?"

"But my father always says the Egyptians just talk babble!" Much appreciative laughter followed his observation.

Chelubai was next to read, and he had chosen the story of Abraham conquering the five kings to rescue his nephew Lot.[25] The boys loved this story and his reading was peppered with, "Only 318 men to fight all those kings?" "Didn't he keep *anything* for himself?" "Tell us more about that Melchizedek!" and "Wow! Isn't Dan way up north?"

As he rolled the scroll and handed it to Betsalel he concluded, "See, God can help you do anything! Never forget, we're the ones who will

23. Gen 18:1–15
24. Gen 11:1–9
25. Gen chapter 14.

conquer Canaan!" There were many cries of "Wow!" "You mean us!" and the like.

Then it was Joel's opportunity. He turned to the story of Joseph interpreting the dreams of the butler and baker which led to his being called to interpret the dreams of none other than the great Pharaoh himself.[26] This brought lots of loud hand clapping and cheering.

Finally, it was Obadiah's turn. "In the beginning," he began, very solemnly, "God created the heavens and the earth. And the earth was without form, and void, and darkness was over the face of the deep. And the Spirit of God was hovering over the face of the waters." As he continued the story of creation week there was not a murmur, not a movement, from the attentive young listeners.[27]

He handed the scroll to Betsalel and there was just one awe-struck exclamation. "We come from God! We always belonged to him!"

"That's right, son, I mean daughter!" grinned Obadiah.

Betsalel waited patiently until the youngsters began moving and chatting, and then he made his little sales talk about teaching those who would like to read. Every hand shot up eagerly. He gave times and venues, and looked as though he was about to dismiss them when Abishua's hand shot up. "Please, Uncle Betsalel, *I* came to hear *your* story! Please tell us! That's how I got all these kids to come. I told them that the tabernacle maker would talk to us."

"Really?" said Betsalel, eyes twinkling.

"Yes, that's what Joel told me, and that's why I'm here." There were many cries of "Yes, yes!"

Betsalel smiled, and sat down on a convenient rock. "You all know I'm just an ordinary fix-it man," he began, but was interrupted.

"No! My mother says you're special. She says you're the most self-controlled, gentle, faithful, good, kind, patient, joyful and loving man she knows.[28] I want to know why and how you are so good!"

"I'm just an ordinary man," began Betsalel, again, smiling. "Some people think because I was in charge of making the tabernacle that I'm special. But no, everyone who allows God to use them can do what he wants. So, let me tell my story.[29]

26. Gen chapters 40 and 41.

27. Gen 1:1—2:3.

28. This is Gal 5:22–23 in reverse. Betsalel is the first person noted in the Bible that God said he would fill with his Spirit.

29. This story is just reasonable conjecture.

Story Time.

"When I was a lad in Egypt, about the same age as you kids, I was very interested in the work my friend's father did. He was a jeweler for the Pharaoh's household. And he made beautiful things, really beautiful things. He noticed I was always hanging around, and one day he made me an offer. He would teach me everything he knew, if I would join his household, become his adopted son. He promised he could get me out of making bricks all day like the other Hebrew people, simply if I would agree."

"Lucky you!" exclaimed a boy at the back of the group, with several agreeing shouts of "yeah!"

"Well, there was a bit of a price to pay, you see, so I didn't."

There was a gasp. "Surely not!" exclaimed the same boy at the back. "Did you really say no to him? I sure wouldn't have been so silly!"

"Well, you see," said Betsalel calmly, "what he wanted me to do was become his adopted son, which meant I would have to worship his gods. He was very clear about that. Give up being an Israelite, and I'll make you an Egyptian, he offered. So I thanked him as politely as I could, but said I could never give up my God."

"Was he angry with you?" a young girl asked.

"I'm afraid he was. He even beat me for being so obstinate. Of course I stopped going to my friend's house. Then one day my friend came and said his father was very sorry for what he had done to me, and even though I would not agree to being adopted by him, I could still come to his place every day after I had done my brick work, and he would show me how to make the beautiful things he did. I must tell you I was very scared going back there, but deep down he was an honest man, just didn't know the true God. He never harmed me again after that. Of course, I was always very tired after making bricks for those cruel taskmasters, and so sometimes I did not learn very fast. But I did go, every day, and did the best I could. He showed me how to mold things in gold and silver, and make intricate patterns. I learned to make wooden frames that could be covered with gold. There was so much to learn, and I wondered if I would ever be able to master it all.

"Then Moses came back to Egypt and you know all about the terrible plagues that happened to the Egyptians."[30] Betsalel paused, and took a very deep breath. There was a catch in his voice as he continued. "Oh, I'm sorry kids. It all happened a long time ago, before any of you were born. Terrible things happened to me in Egypt, really terrible." Betsalel stopped, and his

---

30. Exod.7:14—11:10.

face was twisted with pain. After a few minutes he composed himself and continued, "And in that last plague of Egypt my best friend died. He was the eldest son, you see.[31] I tried to get his father to allow him to stay with me that night, but his father just laughed and said it was all superstitious nonsense, that there was no way every firstborn son could die in one night, and smearing blood on doorposts could never prevent such a ridiculous possibility."

"Didn't even the firstborn animals die?" asked a small boy sitting cross-legged in the front row. "My father says that's why not only are first born children consecrated to God, but also all firstborn animals."[32]

Betsalel looked up, surprised. "You're right!" he agreed. "I'd forgotten the animals! Hope all you firstborn kids know you belong to God!"

Several nodded and smiled proudly.

"Yes, sadly my friend's father just would not listen to me. But when his son did die, like all the other firstborns in Egypt, his father was heartbroken, and he begged me to become his adopted son. But I knew God wanted me to go with his people, so once again I refused him. You see, I had other reasons to know how cruel those Egyptians could be. Even if my friend's father treated me well, I had no guarantee others would. But I confess in all the confusion it was very tempting."

"Was he angry, again?" asked a young man.

"No, not this time. He was just terribly sad, and it was hard, very hard to leave him there in Egypt. I confess I wept. But oh, the incredible freedom of following God. I shall never forget that song we sang on the banks of the Red Sea! Never!"

"That's what my father and grandfather say," agreed Abishua, nodding enthusiastically.

"Being free wasn't that easy at first, after the excitement of having no bricks wore off. I remember all the grumbles about water and food. But I shall never forget discovering the Sabbath through manna. I knew then that following God was very different from the mad race for money and power that was Egyptian life. A God who wanted us to rest and spend time with him was so different from those Egyptian gods that just needed to be pleased all the time."

"Tell us about how you got your job," called a girl from the front row of listeners. "I mean the one with the tabernacle."

31. Exod. 12:29–30
32. Exod. 11:5; 12:29; 13:1

"Yes, that was a shock. I remember so well the time God spoke to us all from the mountain, so scary yet so amazing. Then Moses disappeared up the fiery mountain and we never saw him for forty days. People thought he'd abandoned us, or been killed by the fire, and they got very scared. Some of the people who'd come with us from Egypt suggested they make this calf, and convinced the leaders to help them. Or I should say they convinced one leader. My grandfather Hur had been one of Moses' special helpers, and Moses had left the whole camp to be under the charge of my grandfather and uncle Aaron, the high priest.[33] Aaron is a helpful man, but not so very brave. My grandfather opposed their ideas, and there was a fight, and they killed him."[34] Again Betsalel paused, and blew his nose.

"That must have made you very sad," said Obadiah kindly.

"Yes, it was a great grief, but imagine my shock, when our family was still in mourning, and Moses came to me privately one morning and told me God had called me by name, me and Oholiab, to be the builders of the tabernacle God was talking to Moses about during those forty days he was up the mountain!"

"You must have felt very proud," declared Abishua.

"No son, I didn't. I was shocked, and deeply humbled that it should be me that God knew by name! But I suddenly realized God had been preparing me all along for this stupendous task, why my Egyptian friend's father had taught me the basics of what I needed to know to build what God wanted. Everything fell together, and I was in awe."

"Did God work a miracle and tell you how to do everything?" asked another boy.

"More than a miracle. God filled me with his Spirit,[35] the same Spirit that created the whole world."

"Really? Does that Spirit make you feel sort of different, weird?"

"No, I realized being filled with God's Spirit was simply having God direct my life completely. Moses told me I was the first person he knew about whom God said he would fill with his Spirit, but I know, after we built the tabernacle, and while we were on our way to Kadesh Barnea, and people were complaining and Moses was struggling to cope, God filled

33. Exod. 17:8–13; 24:14.

34. Nothing more is heard of Hur after his commission to lead Israel while Moses was on the mountain for forty days, but there is a Jewish tradition that the reason for this is that Hur was murdered in the conflict over the golden calf. https://www.jewishencyclopedia.com/articles/7942-hur 22 July 2021.

35. Exod. 31:1–6; 35:30–35.

seventy men with his Spirit,[36] so that Moses would have help. I had already learned in Egypt many of the skills I needed to make the things for the tabernacle, but with God everything came together, and I suddenly had the confidence to carry out all those incredible designs God had given Moses on the mountain. You know, nothing beats working with God. In Egypt, working was terrible, yes, slavery. We had no choice but to work, work, work, like it or not, on things other people wanted. But when we built the tabernacle for God it was such fun. And the bit I loved most is that God insisted we still rest even though we were building for him! He was very clear, he still wanted us to rest on the Sabbath![37] He even told us we weren't to light fires, because of course with all the metal working fires were very much part of what we needed for our work! Working for God is very different from working the Egyptian way!"

"So did you really make *It*, I mean *Them*, you know the things we aren't even allowed to see?"

"I guess you mean the ark of the covenant, and the other furniture of the tabernacle?"

The boy nodded. "Weren't you scared?" the boy added.

"No son, I wasn't scared. When you work with God you let him take over. You just do what he asks, and don't worry about anything else."

"Did you make things the way you thought they should look?"

Betsalel smiled. "No, definitely not! I had very careful instructions and plans from Moses, who got the blueprints from God, and I made everything exactly as he had written down. You see, they weren't Moses' plans, they were God's. They were plans that came straight from heaven, God's home."[38]

"So, can you read?"

"Yes, I can. I have a good memory, but being able to read makes knowing what God wants much easier."

"Then I want to learn to read, too," announced a young man sitting beside Obadiah. "Please help us."

Betsalel bowed his head and prayed in wonder and joy, "Oh Yahweh, God of our Fathers, may you be blessed and praised for your kindness to these young people. May they all consecrate their lives to you, and may they be filled with your Spirit as you have done for me."

When he opened his eyes, the whole group was bowed in prayer.

36. Numb.11:14–30.

37. Exod. 35:1–3

38. Exod.25:9.

9

God's Revealing Plans

"How many of you have learned to read?" asked Betsalel, about a year after his successful "story time" initiative. To his delight every hand shot high. "Fantastic!" he grinned. "That means all of you can find out exactly what's inside the sanctuary, and you don't need me to tell you! Moses has written it out most carefully for you."

"But we can't *see* it," complained one of the boys seated expectantly in front of Betsalel. "Why is God so secretive?"

"That's the big problem, son," replied Betsalel. "People want to see God, like we see this rock I'm sitting on, but what he wants is that we believe him, trust him. Because we are sinful, seeing God would simply destroy us. Now, let's go back to the amazing time when people did see the power of God, if not God himself. I was there. How many of your parents have told you what happened that day?"

Abishua's hand shot up. "My father told me many times. He says it was super scary. Lots and lots of fire, lots and lots of noise like thunder on the mountain, and then this amazing, beautiful voice speaking[1] the Ten Words[2] of how we should behave. The voice was magnificent, but it felt as though you could hear it, see it, and feel it, and my father said he was terrified." There were several cries of "Yeah, mine too," and similar.

"That's true," admitted Betsalel, "it *was* scary. Super scary! But it was also wonderful. Moses reminded us that God rescued us from the Egyptian slavery, that he carried us on eagles' wings and brought us to himself. God

1. Exod. 19:18–19; 20:18
2. The Ten Words is the Hebrew way of referring to the Ten Commandments.

offered that if we would cooperate with him and keep his commandments we would be his special people, a holy nation of priests.[3]

"Now we had to prepare ourselves, taking three days to wash and clean everything, ourselves and our clothes. We weren't allowed near the mountain until we had done so. But then, amazingly we learned that when the trumpet sounded we were all, everyone who had prepared themselves, allowed to go near the mountain, the mountain of God!"

"You were actually on the mountain, you yourself?"

"Yes, I truly was, at least, at the bottom of it. When that marvelous voice began the first thing it said was 'I am the LORD your God who brought you out of the land of Egypt, out of the house of bondage.'[4] Before God gave us any rules, or asked us to do anything for him, he reminded us of what he had done for us. And that's what God's always like. He does everything for us, and only asks us to do a few things for him! Now you all know what he asked us to do. The last six commandments are the behavior all of us would want from other people. As for the first four, they might not be so obvious, but when you think of Egypt, you know what having lots of gods does—it causes confusion and lots and lots of rules. But, as you've just told me, instead of concentrating on what God was telling us, we all got scared and just thought of our own safety. I mean, there was God telling us how much he loved us and what he'd done for us, and we were fussing about whether he would destroy us! The fire and the thunder made us think God was there to harm us, as though he would do to us what he had done when he rescued us from those cruel Egyptians! So, instead of listening to God, we asked Moses to do it for us. Moses was very good to us, agreed to help, and even more amazing, God agreed to let him![5] God talked to Moses and Moses carefully wrote down everything God said, read it all out to us, and gave us the chance to agree or disagree.[6] There was lots of emphasis on treating other people nicely, people like foreigners and widows and slaves, although God did have rules about how he wanted us to worship him.[7] He obviously did not like Egyptian-style worship! He finished by promising he would help us conquer Canaan.[8] Then everyone said, twice,

3. Exod.19:5–6
4. Exod. 20:2
5. Exod. 20:18–21
6. Exod. 24:4,7
7. Exod. 20:22—23:19.
8. Exod. 23:20–33

'All that the Lord has said we will do.' There was no mistaking what they said! Then Moses threw the blood of the covenant over us. It was amazing, very emotional. We knew we were now really God's people."[9]

"Did you get any blood of the covenant on you?"

"Yes, I did. We all wanted that blood when Moses threw it over us. Young and old, we rushed forward to become part of God's covenant. Some people even compared how much blood they received, but that was foolish behavior."

"So God actually kept on giving some rules to Moses after the Ten Words?" asked a pretty young woman, eyes wide with surprise.

"He did. What he gave were various explanations about the Ten Words, all very understandable, and Moses recorded them for us. At the end of that amazing ceremony God invited Moses, Aaron, Nadab and Abihu and seventy of the elders of Israel to come right up on the mountain, and they ate a meal and saw God! What they saw was the pavement under his feet, which was the splendid color of lapis lazuli."[10]

"Oh, wow!" "That's amazing!" "Lapis lazuli is such a wonderful blue!" "Did they *really* have a meal with God?" "Have you talked with any of those people?" "They didn't die on the mountain?" The chorus of responses continued for several minutes.

Betsalel waited until all exclamations of wonder ceased before beginning to share what Moses had learned when he went back up the mountain on his own, during the next forty days.

"Yes, those men really did eat on the mountain with God. I talked to my grandfather Hur about it, and he trembled with awe and excitement as he told me. But when Moses went back up the mountain to talk with God, he left my grandfather and Aaron in charge of the people.[11] It was while Moses was up on the mountain that God told him how to make the tabernacle. Everyone is interested in what's inside the tabernacle, and some of you think I'm special because I've actually seen it, handled it, made it. I tell you all the things in the sanctuary are very beautiful, glimmering, glistening, shimmering with gold. But lots of people saw what I was making. It was no secret! The things I made are simple, and you can read about them.

9. Exod. 24:3–8

10. Exod. 24:9–11. The "sapphire" of most translations actually means the beautiful blue rock lapis lazuli. Sapphire as a gemstone was not known until Roman times.

11. Exod. 24:12–18

Actually, there were many of us involved in making the sanctuary.[12] It was a wonderful community activity. Lots of people gave gifts, so many gifts that those of us making things had to tell Moses to stop people bringing more contributions![13] So many people assisted making the tabernacle, women as well as men.[14] So many were willing, not just willing but eager, to do what God wanted them to do! I tell you, it was all a lot of fun. It was a wonderful time working together.

"What was most amazing is that God showed Moses a pattern, a blueprint of the sanctuary, a blueprint that represents God's home in heaven. The ark of the covenant, made of gold-covered acacia wood, with two glorious solid gold cherubim and the solid gold mercy seat above it,[15] is in the Most Holy Place that only the high priest enters once a year on the Day of Atonement.[16] That Most Holy Place is a miniature of God's throne room. Inside the ark are the second tables of stone that God asked Moses to make after the horrible molten calf situation,[17] with the Ten Words written on them, and that's why it's often called the ark of the covenant. Beside the ark are two interesting things: a pot of manna that has never got smelly,[18] and the rod of Aaron that grew flowers and fruit overnight, to prove he was God's choice for the priesthood.[19] Beside the Most Holy Place is the Holy Place. Priests go into the Holy Place every day. It too has walls covered with gold, and there are three things in there: a candlestick of pure gold, with seven branches to give light and it symbolizes the spiritual wisdom of understanding[20], a golden table with very simple unleavened bread that is changed every week, and bowls for drink offerings[21], and a small golden altar for incense.[22] The lamp is amazing. It's made of pure gold and weighs

12. Exod. 35:10

13. Exod.35:4–9, 20–24; 36:2–7

14. Exod. 35:10, 25–26

15. Exod. 25:10–22

16. See Lev. Chapter 16

17. Exod.34:1

18. Exod. 16:33–34

19. Numb. 17:10–11

20. Exod. 25:31–39

21. Exod. 25:23–30

22. Exod. 30:1–10

a whole talent,[23] which is more than most of you weigh, and about half as much as me!"

"I thought the tabernacle would all be full of fancy carvings, things like the Egyptians had," observed a tall young man at the back, but Betsalel shook his head gently. "I can tell you everything is incredibly beautiful, but very simple."

Some of his audience were clearly not impressed with the idea of simplicity, but others were pensively awed.

"Now I want to tell you some amazing things I discovered when Moses gave me the plans for the building of the sanctuary. Moses wrote out very carefully what God told him, just as God shared it with him. So I discovered God had spoken to Moses seven different times while he was there on the mountain.[24] When we look at those seven speeches from God we can see something remarkable." Betsalel stopped, and looked at Jahath and Chelubai who were seated beside him. "You remember Phinehas' consecration service?" he asked them. "How he told us that for him the most emotional part was having the powerful, sweet-smelling and fragrant sacred oil poured on him? Well, that anointing oil is right in the center of the seven speeches from God!"[25]

"Wow! That's amazing? Does Phinehas know that?" asked Chelubai. "I remember he was very impressed with the beautiful perfume of the holy oil. He said it penetrated everything, as though God was sealing him right through to his bones as God's very own possession."

"Yes, I remember how excited Phinehas was about that oil. It's the oil that makes things holy, isn't it?" asked Jahath eagerly.

Betsalel nodded. "The oil is important, but it's what it symbolizes that counts. It means a person, or a thing, belongs to God."

"So what were the other speeches about?" added Abishua, wriggling his feet in the sand.

"Well, the first and longest speech is all about the tabernacle and the priests and their consecration. And the last speech is about the Sabbath."[26]

"Does that mean the Sabbath is as important as the sanctuary?" asked Abishua incredulously. "I thought it was just a day to have a rest."

23. Exod. 25:39. A talent was about 34 kgs.

24. Exod. 25:1, 30:11, 30:17, 30:22, 30:34, 31:1, 31:12

25. What is described here is classical chiastic structure, a common, elegant, and very effective form of ancient writing. The oil is described in Exod.30:22–33

26. Exod. 25:10—30:10 and Exod. 31:12–17.

"Well, it seems from God's point of view the Sabbath and the sanctuary are both very important. The sanctuary is the *place* we meet God, and the Sabbath is the *time* we spend with him. You'll notice that God wants us to meet with him very frequently, once every seven days, so that means the Sabbath is pretty important. What I like about all of this is that God is not haphazard. He presents things in a wonderfully orderly way. The speech about the Sabbath is a little scary because it says if we don't keep the Sabbath we will die. But God is trying to help us understand that he is the One that gives us life. If we cut ourselves off from God, then of course we will eventually die, like those Egyptian firstborn."

"Is this dying like the dying that was promised in that garden with the mean snake?" asked Abishua. "I mean, they didn't die immediately, but they did die eventually, didn't they?"

"Very true, son," smiled Phineas. "When we don't listen to God we cut ourselves off from him, which of course means we will eventually die."

A solemn pause followed these thoughts, while everyone pondered this serious idea.

Then suddenly Betsalel shocked everyone and began to laugh. "It was when I saw what God had paired up next that I realized I truly wasn't very important after all! God made a special speech about me, the sixth, but the second speech that partners with the speech about me and Oholiab is all about atonement money that shows everyone over the age of twenty is worth exactly the same amount as everyone else! Now, that's truly amazing. Of course, most people don't like tax, but a tax that keeps God's house in repair and makes everyone equal is very special. This tax is nothing like the Egyptian way of taking tax money to show that some people are more important than others. In God's eyes we're all equal. Being called by God is a privilege and a responsibility, but it doesn't make a person better than anyone else!"[27]

"Hey, that's really neat," butted in Kenaz. "You know, I've always had the silly idea that somehow you were better than me, but now you've just shown me that's wrong. God thinks we're equal."

"Exactly! He certainly does! See what I mean?" insisted Betsalel. "God thinks of everything. We just have to read carefully! Trouble is most of us are in too much hurry, and we think we know what's written when we've hardly looked. So, yes, it was very humbling, but also inspiring, when I realized God thinks of us all as valuable, equally valuable. Anyway, the final

27. See Exod. 30:11–16 and 31:1–11.

pair is the bronze washing basin and the incense. I'm not yet sure what that means, but since God wants us all to be his holy people, a holy nation,[28] washing in that basin and the billowing incense must be ways of helping us become holy. I am sure with time God will reveal to us all just what all the parts of the sanctuary mean."[29]

"That's amazing," declared a young man sitting on the edge of the group, clearly not quite sure if he belonged or not. "I always thought the tabernacle was just about that blood and gore stuff to keep the priests busy and stops God getting angry. I had no idea it was God teaching us about himself, and wanting me to be a holy person for him. I'm going to have to rethink everything!"

"Do that son!" exclaimed Betsalel joyfully. "The more you think the more you'll like it!"

"But why did God have to make one speech so long, and some so short?" asked Abishua. "You say he remembers everything, but it seems he just added bits at the end that he'd forgotten."

"Now, here's another nice thing I wanted to tell you. I've shared how God's speeches make a sort of envelope, and we can learn a great deal from the arrangement of those seven speeches. Now that long first speech also has a nice pattern, a similar idea to what I've just shared with you."

"What, more holiness in the middle?"

"No, I've got another surprise for you! That long speech has eleven parts, the same number of parts as the First Book of Moses, which is interesting.[30] I hope you are all reading from that book, and discovering where we come from as a people. Anyway, the first part of God's long speech is all about people giving things to God so the sanctuary can be built,[31] and the last part is all about the altar of incense.[32] That was a big surprise to me. Moses had talked to me about the plans, but when I came to read them, I really thought either Moses or God had forgotten to include the altar of incense. I was going to tease him about forgetting, but when I read carefully I realized no, God was telling me something special in the arrangement

---

28. Exod.19:6

29. This hints that not everything would have been clear to the Children of Israel in the wilderness. With Christian hindsight we can see these parts of the tabernacle service represent the cleansing of baptism and the ascending incense indicates prayer.

30. The book of Genesis is arranged as eleven *toledoth* or generation sections.

31. Exod.25:1–7

32. Exod. 30:1–10

of the first long speech that reveals his love and his plans. So, I think this means while we can give God our things, our money and our time, he is the one who gives us holiness from the smell of the incense. But the altar of incense is very close to the ark of the covenant, so maybe the incense is a symbol of us coming close to God and getting to know him as we give our things and hearts to him. I like to think of it as our privilege of actually talking to God in prayer."

There was a long pause while Betsalel appeared to contemplate what else the incense might mean. Finally he continued, "I discovered the next two parts were all about what God wanted the sanctuary for, the purpose of it all. That was very exciting! The second part tells us simply that God wants to live with us[33], but the tenth part is more specific, telling us God wants to meet with us, consecrate us, live with us, and simply be our God.[34] Don't you think that's amazing? Instead of just telling us what he wants, he tells us how much he wants us! We started this discussion with how scary God seemed to be up on that mountain, but as I studied the plans for the tabernacle I realized God *loves* us, and *wants* us. I'm awed by our God!"

A young boy beside Abishua frowned. "I confess I'm finding this all rather confusing. You'll have to explain it to us better."

"Let me tell you, I'm still learning what the sanctuary can teach me about God. But I'll try to make it more simple for you."

Betsalel turned around, and grabbing Jahath's brand new walking staff, began to write in the sand at their feet. "First, I'll show you about the seven speeches. Here they are:

"1. The sanctuary and its furniture
2. The atonement money
3. The Bronze basin
4. The Anointing oil
5. The Incense
6. The Call of Betsalel and Oholiab
7. The Sabbath."[35]

Obadiah sat up, spoke up. "You know, I thought these sessions were for these youngsters, but I'm learning heaps! Do you think God thought all this out, or Moses?"

---

33. Exod. 25:8
34. Exod. 29:42–46
35. Exod. 25:1—31:17. The seven speeches each begin with "The Lord said to Moses".

"Moses told me it was God who inspired him with what to write, and how to write it. Moses used his own words, but they were God's ideas. When I look at the world around me, things like leaves, and birds, and shells, I know God likes patterns. So I think the patterns in the sanctuary plans were God's idea."

"Either way, it's amazing!" exclaimed Obadiah.

"But, I have more good things I've learned. You won't be surprised to hear that God next talks about the furniture of the sanctuary, the ark of the covenant, the table for the bread, and the lamp,[36] but what delighted me was this paired up with the consecration of the priests.[37] So all those special holy things inside the tabernacle, things you kids are so keen to see, actually match up with the priests that you *can see* walking around all the time! So, it's not just 'stuff' that is special and holy, but people and the work they do!"

"I never thought of the priests being as important as the furniture!" exclaimed Abitub.

"It's an incredible thought, isn't it?" agreed Betsalel. "By now I don't think you'll be a bit surprised to discover that the walls and coverings of the tabernacle[38] are paired with the clothes of the priests.[39] Interesting, the coverings for the tent are very beautiful on the inside but very plain on the outside, but for the priests, especially the high priest, it's the other way around. Anyone any suggestions why that might be?"

There was a long silence, and then a rather scared-looking girl raised her hand. "Do you think," she began timidly, "I mean, is it possible it's because God has to cover his holiness so he won't scare us, but we have to cover up our messiness and wickedness with his holiness on the outside?"

Betsalel looked at the frightened young girl in amazement. "That's a wonderful idea!" he exclaimed. "That's just perfect! Thank you for helping me understand more of God's goodness!" The girl blushed deeply, but smiled jubilantly.

"Did you all hear that?" Betsalel asked, turning to the whole group. "If you think the tabernacle doesn't look very pretty with its plain leather covering, remember God is hiding his glory for you. But he hides the priests' messy humanness with his beautiful clothes. Isn't that amazing!" He paused. Some nodded with understanding, some looked blank.

36. Exod. 25:10–40
37. Exod. 29:1–35
38. Exod. 26:1–37
39. Exod. 28:1–43

"Well, we've only two more layers to go! Next we have the bronze altar of sacrifice[40] that teams up with the description of the oil for the lamp.[41] I really prayed about what these might mean, because they appear so different. As I was praying God impressed my heart that these two represent how God works for us. Kenaz and Jahath and Chelubai, and of course Obadiah and Joel, will remember years ago I shared something Moses told me: when we offer a sin offering on the bronze altar and the blood of the sacrifice is applied to the altar, it shows God actually carries the burden of our guilt and shame, and we can lift it all on to him. Now I still don't understand that completely, but it's a wonderful picture of what the altar represents for us. And of course the oil is what makes the lamp give its light, it's the power of the lamp. So, I think God is telling us the work he does for us is first that he will carry our sins away from us and give us peace, and then he gives us his wisdom and his light of understanding so we can live the way he wants us to live, according to those Ten Words. I think that's what God gave me when he sent his Spirit to help me, to empower me, know how to build his tabernacle."

"Oh wow! And I thought all that stuff was just a set of builders' instructions!" Chelubai clapped his hands to his forehead in mock dismay, but real amazement. "But it's still a bit confusing! I wonder how many of these kids understand!"

"Let me write out the plan for the tabernacle blueprint. Here it is." Again Betsalel wrote in the sand with the Jahath's rod.

"1. The People's Freewill offering.
    2. The Purpose of it All
        3. The Furniture of God's House
            4. The Walls and Coverings of the Tabernacle
                5. The Bronze Altar
                    6. The Court of the Tabernacle
                7. Oil for the Lamp
            8. Priestly Garments
        9. Consecration of Priests
      10. The Purpose of it all
    11. The Altar of Incense." (Exod. 25:1—30:9)

---

40. Exod. 27:1-8
41. Exod. 27:20-21

Sanctuary and Furniture
Atonement money
Bronze basin
Anointing Oil
Incense
Call of Betsalel and Oholiab
Sabbath

People's Freewill Offering
Purpose of it all
Furniture of God's house
Wall of Tabenacle
Bronze Altar
Court of Taberacle
Oil for lamp
Priestly Clothes
Consecration of Priests
Purpose of all
Altar of incense

Everything Has Meaning.

"I confess at the beginning I too thought it was just builder's plans. But careful study has made me realize it is much, much more. And now for the middle!" Betsalel paused, as though trying to understand the full import of his own discovery. "God is so loving. You know, can you see, right in the center of all those builder's instructions, in the middle of all those magnificent things, is simply the description of the courtyard where all God's people can come! Anyone can come to him there! Can you believe it? He puts us at the center of everything!" Betsalel used the rod to draw a circle around the words "Court of the Tabernacle".

"You mean, we're at the center of God's thinking?" exclaimed a small boy.

"So it isn't all just about him, it's about us too?" asked another wide-eyed lad.

"Well, it's not that we're so marvelous, but that God loves us so much! Think of it this way," replied Betsalel. "It's all about God wanting to meet with us so he can become our friend, and for us to get to know him better."

"This can't be right! Why all the gore?" demanded a disheveled boy at the back. "Isn't God just a sadist?"

There was a shocked silence following this angry declaration. After Betsalel's talking about God loving people, it jarred in everyone's mind to hear God called a sadist.

"Think of it like this," answered Betsalel, gently smiling at the angry, posturing young man. "Does God ever sprinkle any of that gore on *our* clothes? Does he ever ask us to take home that horrible gore to mess up *our* tents with blood, or is it his house and his representatives the priests that carry all of that mess, for us?"

The lad dropped his gaze, and muttered sullenly, "So he takes the blame for all my blunders? He carries all the burden of the troubles I cause? I just can't believe that nonsense!"

"Simply, trust me," smiled Betsalel, "the answer is yes. God is willing to carry our burdens, *all* our burdens, all the horrible gore of our mistakes, our sins!"

The disheveled boy turned pale, and sat down suddenly.

"Hey! Why don't you come with me to the tent and make a sin offering with me," pled another boy beside the disheveled lad, nudging his angry friend urgently. "Don't you think it would be much better to give God our problem, than to continue always feeling bad about it ourselves?"

"I'll think about it," said the boy, but his voice was no longer as defiant.

"You never mentioned anything about dedicating the whole thing," asked a puzzled young man. "Wouldn't that be important?"

"You're right! It *was* important. God gave very clear instructions about that, after we had made everything according to God's instructions, and Moses set it all up. As I said, God didn't forget anything, but perhaps he had to make sure we obeyed first and did as he asked before we needed to know about the dedication. But it was amazing when everything was finished, and Moses had checked everything and set it all up, *then* the anointing oil was poured over everything. The perfume of that oil filled the whole camp for days. Let me tell you Moses was very, very fussy about checking everything, to make sure we had done exactly what God had planned. Then the cloud came and covered the tent of meeting, and God's glory filled the tabernacle, so that not even Moses could go in. I will never forget that moment!"[42]

"Betsalel," said Kenaz when the look of supreme awe on Betsalel's face had faded, "I'm ashamed to admit I've been one of those people who thought we should be allowed to have a look inside that Holy Place. But when I realize God's glory is so great even Moses can be excluded sometimes, I stand in absolute amazement that God is willing to be in our camp, present with us, at all."

"So it's not all just gore and blood and sin?" a small lad at the back of the group called.

"It's about God himself," replied Betsalel, in a reverent whisper. "And what he does for us."

"I thought it was simply how we could stop him getting angry with us. I mean, that's what the Egyptians told me about their religious festivals. All that scary stuff up on the mountain when the Ten Words were given, and the all the fuss about the golden calf sounds like God can get cross very easily and destroy us for the least little thing." The young questioner was clearly very troubled.

"Doesn't all that gore and killing mean God is angry all the time?" asked another boy, frowning. "Aren't our offerings to appease him, to stop him getting mad like he did with those Egyptians?"

Betsalel shook his head vigorously. "Please, talk to each other about all that I have shared with you," he pled. "I'll try to think of other ways to make it easier for you to understand."

"While we're talking about sin and all that horrible stuff," said a rather prim young woman, "can you explain what *was* the big deal with that golden

42. Exod.40:1–35

105

calf story? I've asked my father about it numerous times, but he always just walks away and says, 'Just be glad I didn't get killed.' It seems God gets mad for every tiny mistake!"

"Yes, we can talk about that, but I think it better be next time," smiled Betsalel. "Just remember, the tabernacle is about God. So if you can't understand something, don't get too concerned. I mean, how can any of us ever truly understand God himself?"

Betsalel frowned thoughtfully, as the youngsters slowly got up to leave. "You know," he sighed, "there's so much to learn. But I'll try very hard to make it easy for you."

"Look forward to next time," said Joel.

10

When God Carries the Load

When the group next met both key speakers and audience were surprised.

Many of the youth in the group Jahath, Chelubai, and Kenaz led, once they had learned to read and write, stopped attending meetings. The numbers dwindled to fifteen. Betsalel was disappointed, but still believed God had called him to teach. One of the best leaders in the group proved to be Jeriel, from the tribe of Issachar, the disheveled lad who had once scathingly called God a sadist. He and his friend Izrahiah[1] gathered their courage, begged a lamb from Izrahiah's father, which they took to Phinehas, who gently helped them understand what a sin offering meant, and helped them offer the lamb for their part in stealing some fine clothes from a neighbor. They returned the clothes to the rightful owner, who graciously insisted that because they were young they did not need to add anything to its value, even though it was the law to do so.[2] They were delighted when Moses agreed. Now they frequently, with tears in their eyes, talked about what they called their *keseblelohim*[3] "lamb of God", that had taken away their terrible sense of guilt and shame.

But, today, when Betsalel arrived at the usual meeting venue under the luxuriant spreading terebinths, there were not fifteen youngsters waiting, but all the new groups plus originals, making almost one hundred people!

---

1. Jeriel and Izrahiah are names taken from those in the tribe of Issachar, 1 Chon 7:1–3

2. Lev 5:14–16

3. *keseb* is Hebrew for lamb, and *elohim* for God.

Smiling mischievously were Abitub and Elpaal with their group, Oholiab and his brother with theirs, and Assir, Mishael, and Mikael with their discussion class. But these eager learners were equally surprised when they realized they were not only meeting with their beloved Betsalel, but Moses had come to speak with them as well. The topic of the terrible molten calf tragedy was clearly of great interest to them all, and who better than Moses to explain what happened?

"It's God-ordained," murmured Moses, as he and Betsalel neared the group. "His Spirit must have spoken to all of them. You tell them what it was like waiting for me when I was up the mountain, and how things started, and I'll go on from there."

"Certainly," agreed Betsalel, and turning to the group said, with the broadest smile, "This is a big surprise! I can't tell you how happy it makes me to see all of you!"

"And we you!" called dozens of eager voices.

"Well, today Moses and I want to share with you the worst of stories, and the best of news. How does that sound?" Much eager nodding followed. "Perhaps some of your parents have told you about the day of the calf . . ."

"No!" called Jeriel. "No one I asked would talk about it. They'd say things like 'best you don't know' or 'it just happened once so forget it' or the worst excuse, for me, 'you're too young to understand!'"

"It's such a pity parents don't talk to their children about things they should know, even bad things. Secrets are dangerous, and only prolong problems. That's why I've spent so much time writing the truth about our people and the laws God gave us," Moses responded to Betsalel quietly. "I pray my writing will allow everyone to know the truth about what happened, not only with that calf, but what God did for us all though our wanderings."

Betsalel nodded, then turning to the group he said, "I'm really sorry to hear that, Jeriel. You're certainly old enough to understand! So I'll start from the beginning. After God spoke with us from the mountain and gave us his laws, we had that incredible covenant-confirming ceremony I told you about last time. We all felt pretty good, very proud of ourselves. We were the special people of God, we would do exactly what he told us, and we'd soon be in that Promised Land flowing with milk and honey.[4] Moses was up and down the mountain so many times that no one was even slightly concerned when he went back up there after the covenant cutting

4. Exod. 3:8

ceremony.[5] For a few days there was a lot of interest in comparing the blood on our clothes, the bigger the spot, the prouder the owner. Now, these days, of course, it's the priests who have their clothes spotted with the blood of sacrifices.

"But soon the blood-spotting pastime lost its interest. The women swapped manna recipes, but quickly ran out of ideas. When Moses had not appeared after a week, people were concerned. At the end of two weeks everyone was worried, not so much about Moses but about what was going to happen to them in the desert. They thought Moses was great when he led them where they wanted to go, but when he went off by himself to talk with God they lost interest, and worse, were afraid. We all felt the power of the fire on the day God spoke, and after much scholarly discussion, we assumed God had simply consumed Moses in his fire. I'm afraid most of us thought it was Moses who brought us out of Egypt, although I'm not sure who we thought we were singing to, or what we were singing about on the side of the Red Sea! I mean, who can make water part and people just walk through like we did![6] Yet lots of us thought it was Moses' magic powers from God that made the Red Sea divide. I'm ashamed to say that we thought that somehow God was an amazing something Moses owned, and without Moses we didn't really know who God was. The big issue became finding a strong leader to direct the camp and take it on its way. But, let me really emphasize, it is *not* a good leader we need to follow, but God himself. Following a leader, even a very good, godly one, rather than following God, is a very serious mistake.

"Importantly, we actually did have two appointed leaders, Aaron and Hur, and they didn't share the anxiety of the crowd, but insisted Moses would return in due time. There was lots of yelling and arguing, and demands that a 'good' leader be found, someone who would do something, and now! Not two useless ones who were not prepared to do anything except sit around and wait. People wanted to be given a definite time for Moses' return, and because Aaron and Hur could not, or would not, give this time, they insisted they were not true leaders. I guess because we had all spent so much time in Egypt we were used to someone yelling at us and directing us. We were not used to waiting for anything, or thinking for ourselves. We should have realized that the appointment of Aaron and Hur

5. Hebrews speak of "cutting" in blood a covenant or agreement, not signing it as in modern parlance.

6. Exod.14:5—5:18

meant Moses expected to be a good time up the mountain, and they were the ones we should respect. But the people didn't think, we didn't think. I've told some of you, now all of you, that my grandfather Hur dared to oppose this idea of finding a new leader, and he opposed even more vigorously the idea that they should make a tangible symbol of God to worship. He insisted God had put him and Aaron in charge, and they would prayerfully do what Moses had asked them to do. But this made the distraught people even more angry and a terrible fight broke out. Standing up for God cost my grandfather his life; he was killed by the mob."[7]

Betsalel paused, sighed deeply, and shook his head sadly.

"My grandfather's death must have made Aaron very frightened, because now he had to face the mob alone. Anyway, after that Aaron was so afraid of the people he agreed to do whatever they wanted. The first thing they organized was a party, a big religious celebration. Many people in the camp, especially the Egyptians who had come with us, were experts in brewing strong drink, called beer. It's a drink made of fermented grains.[8] The Egyptians used this to make their parties wild, full of false courage, and emotional excitement. You know some people in our camp have made this drink, and caused big trouble for themselves and everyone around them. The people also decided they needed some divine help, and should make a representative of the god of heaven, which in Egypt is often made in the likeness of a cow. With Aaron as a helpful, compliant, human leader, lots of jewelry was donated, and the people talked him into making a calf as a representative of God. There was lots of fire, heating, and hammering."

Betsalel again paused, and gave a wry smile before he began chuckling. "You know," he continued, "none of them knew how to work with metals, and that calf they made was the worst replica of a cow that I have ever seen!"[9]

7. This is a well-known tradition of Jewish people, see chapter 7. Certainly Hur is never mentioned in scripture after his appointment as leader while Moses went up to God on the mountain. It is only Aaron who Moses confronted when he returned from the mountain's summit. It is slightly possible that Hur agreed with the calf-making, and was one of the 3,000 killed by loyal Levites, but this seems unlikely, Exod. 32:25–28.

8. https://www.worldhistory.org/article/1033/beer-in-ancient-egypt/ July 23, 2021

9. Casting metal is a time consuming art. This assertion about poor quality is based on the fact that even if the people began making the image as soon as Moses left, time would have restricted the quality of the image produced. Aaron's plea that he "threw the gold in the fire" also suggests hasty workmanship, see Exod. 32:24

There was a ripple of laughter through the crowd, then a friend of Abishua, not impressed, exclaimed, "But why didn't they get you to help, Betsalel? After all, you're the expert, aren't you?"

Betsalel shook his head, and smiled ruefully. "God was merciful to me, and at that time no one knew I had any skills. In fact, I don't think I had any at that time, because God had not yet filled me with his Spirit. Many of the people in the camp did not join in with the rebels, and as long as we kept silent in our tents we thought we were safe. How cowardly we all were! But there was no silencing the huge crash when Moses hurled the beautiful tables of stone that God had given him, and they shattered into a million pieces at the foot of the mountain!" Betsalel sat down abruptly, shuddering.

"It was a terrible sight," continued Moses, rising to his feet. "Joshua, who was with me on the mountain, was absolutely horrified and could not believe his eyes. About 3,000 men full of beery Egyptian courage, many naked, were dancing around this lopsided creature crudely balanced on a rock. I grabbed that pathetic image and immediately ordered that it be ground to dust (never mind it was made of precious metals!) and poured into the drinking stream. Then I made straight for Aaron. He was almost incoherent with shame and maybe even beer, and clearly no use to anyone. Unbelievably, he tried to tell me that all he did was throw some jewelry into the fire, and out popped the calf![10] How could he possibly think I would believe him! So I called for anyone who was on God's side, and was greatly encouraged when all the tribe of Levi gathered around me. They buckled their swords, and went off slaughtering anyone who remained disgracefully defiant. It was a terrible scene."[11] Tears slid down Moses' face. His clear, century-old eyes looked out boldly over the tough terrain of the desert, while he wept softly.

"We slaughtered them," he said sorrowfully, "but I loved them. I pled with God, I pled with all my heart that he would take my life in exchange for them, and forgive them, but God would not accept my offer.[12] He even offered to start all over again and make a new nation from me, me, Moses, who was supposed to deliver them from Egypt![13] But I knew that my sons and their sons would be no better. The whole human race has sold itself to sin, and only God can save us. Now that is the good news I've come to

10. Exod. 32:21–24.
11. Exod. 32:25–29.
12. Exod. 32:30–34
13. Exod. 32:10

share! But there was one person I did save. I pled with God not to destroy my brother, and he listened."[14]

Moses pulled himself together and smiled weakly at the rows of dumbfounded youth sitting cross-legged in front of him. Moses had always seemed so strong and stern. The last thing any of them expected was to see him weep. In embarrassed silence they waited patiently, glad when he continued.

"When God spoke to us in fire and thunder on the mountain he gave us a choice. God never forces. We, the children of Israel, actively chose to work with God, to cut his covenant. Three times all the people said, 'All that the Lord has said, we will do!'[15] No one forced them to say that. But now the covenant was shattered, utterly broken. I mean, what man takes back a woman who has cheated on him? None of us could expect any mercy from God. He generously offered to send his angel to go with us when we headed off for Canaan, but refused to go with us himself because his mere holy presence would destroy us all.[16] I was devastated by the news that God would not go with us, and desperately needed to talk to God, to see him and to try to understand what he really thought. So once more I pleaded with God. I knew how patient he'd been with me, so I did some bargaining. I said, 'You said, I have found grace in your sight. If that's true, show me your way, so I'll really know I've found grace in your sight.' Then he said wonderful words 'My presence *will* go with you and I *will* give you rest.' But I wanted to be really sure. I told him the only way people would know we had found grace was if he went with us, and the Lord again told me 'he knew me by name and I'd found grace in his sight.' So I took courage, and pleaded with God to let me see him, just once *really* see him. Unbelievably, he said I could see his back, and as he passed he would protect me from his full glory with his hand, while I hid in the cleft of the rock."[17]

Moses paused, and his face glowed with joy. "Next morning I went back up that mountain, again. And you know what? I never saw any glory at all! No fire, no thunder, no lightning! I felt Yahweh push me into a cleft in the rock, and as he passed by he *did* cover me with his hand. Then I heard a most melodious voice describe the goodness of God. Oh, the incredible goodness and mercy of God! The voice said, 'The LORD, the LORD, a God

14. Deut. 9:20
15. Exod. 19:8, 24:3, 7.
16. Exod. 33:1–3.
17. Exod. 33:12–23

merciful and gracious, slow to anger and abounding in steadfast love and faithfulness, keeping steadfast love for thousands, forgiving iniquity and transgression and sin, but who will by no means clear the guilty.'[18] It was amazing: after all those people had done, there was God talking to me about mercy!"

Again Moses paused, and his old eyes peered over the youthful audience and across the wide sweeps of desert, as though he was still trying to see God.

"But it was not just forgiveness he was talking about. I heard God say he would *nasa* our mistakes, that is, he would carry them for us like we carry loads of wood and water.[19] When I first shared this with Betsalel he was stunned by God's goodness. He shared this with some of you, am I right? That didn't seem fair to me, to allow God to carry the burden when we'd made the mistake. I wanted God to pardon us,[20] to wipe everything out, give us a clean bowl with no dirt, but God ignored that request. Now I know that idea was impossible. Think of me. I'm a murderer, and nothing can change that except God's mercy. Clearly, God has to keep on carrying our loads of troubles for us until he can dump it all where it belongs and gets rid of it all forever."

"That's not fair," someone murmured. "God shouldn't have to do that!"

"Well, after all that God stunned me. I forgot to tell you that when God allowed me back up the mountain to talk to him he asked me to cut two more tables of stone. That made me feel good, as I was sure that meant God would renew the covenant with us, although as I said, I could hardly believe he would do that, any more than a man will take back a cheating wife, especially one who has made a terrible public display of her behavior. Well, after God declared all his goodness, and said he would carry our load of guilt, but apparently ignored my plea for pardon, he said something astonishing. Yes, he was going to cut a covenant with us, but this one would be a marvel, a miracle, a *pala*. But he was going to *bara* this miracle, and make a new covenant with us!

"Did you hear that! Really hear? This means what God did was utterly new, like when he created, *bara,* the heavens and the earth from nothing.[21]

18. Exod. 34:6–7

19. Exod. 34:7

20. Exod. 34:9

21. Exod. 34:10, Gen 1:1. Usual translations of the Hebrew of Ex 34:10 do not bring out the idea that God was creating something absolutely new, that it was a miracle. But it

He was creating a miracle of forgiveness, and would carry our load of sin! We thought we were making an agreement with God, two equals bargaining with each other and agreeing on the terms of a contract. How incredibly foolish! But now I realized God really, truly, meant what he said, that he would carry the *whole* load of the agreement, and all we could do was respond gratefully to his amazing love!

"Let's get this straight. God was *not* saying we could do what we like and he would close his eyes to our behavior. He will only carry the load of our guilt if we give it to him, and admit he needs to carry it. That means we need to be truly sorry for our bad behavior. Anyway, after telling me about this new covenant God immediately went on to talk about his rules, so obviously they weren't forgotten or wiped out. He specifically mentioned three of them: no idols, no other gods, and keeping the Sabbath.[22] So it was clear that although God was going to carry the load, we had to respect his requirements, the same ones he had given us when he spoke on the mountain and wrote the Ten Words."

Moses stretched his legs. Several of his audience got up and walked around. When everyone was comfortable and reseated, Moses began again.

"I've told you all about that sad molten calf business, but I'm sure you're wondering why was I up the mountain for so long? I hope you know I was originally there for forty days because God was sharing with me the construction plans for the tabernacle he wanted built in the middle of our camp, the wonderful symbol of his perpetual, personal presence. I know Betsalel has told you how he made that incredible house for God, but I want to mention something God added on that amazing interview I had with him after the golden calf misery. He reminded me that he wanted his people to get together three times a year for special feasts. You all know those three times are Passover, the Feast of Weeks, and the Feast of Harvest's end.[23] Now, think about the three apartments in the sanctuary, and see if you can see how those three festivals match up with the three parts of the tabernacle."

The young audience fidgeted, stretched limbs, and many eyes peered vacantly across the vast sweeps of wilderness, mentally groping for inspiration.

---

is clearly in the Hebrew words of the text as noted. It was a *new covenant* based on mercy, not performance.

22. Exod. 34:11, 14, 17, 21.

23. Exod. 34:18–20, 22–23

Carrying Heavy Burdens.

"Since the first Passovers in Egypt and Sinai[24] we haven't kept those feasts, so how can we know what they mean?" muttered Abitub to Kenaz. "These youngsters won't have a clue what they mean!"

"They might surprise us," whispered Kenaz.

Slowly Jeriel raised his hand, then stood. "Yes, son?" said Moses.

"Uncle Moses, when Betsalel told us about making the sanctuary he said God spoke to you seven times on the mountain. Is that true?"

"It certainly is, son."

"Well, he said the first speech was all about the plans for the sanctuary furniture and priests, and the last one was about the Sabbath. He said the sanctuary was the *place* for worshiping God, but the Sabbath was the *time*."

"Absolutely right, my lad."

"Well, this might be a crazy idea. But I was thinking maybe the three parts of the tabernacle building match the three times a year we are supposed to celebrate, and well, learn about God, although I am not quite sure what it all means."

With every word Jeriel uttered Moses became more excited. "You're on to it, son!" he exclaimed.

Jeriel hesitated, then continued. "You see, in both Passover and the altar of burnt offering in the courtyard God takes the load of sin from us. Those animals have to die to show us what God is doing for us, although I can't possibly imagine God would ever die for us. In the Holy Place there is light to give understanding, and bread to nourish us, and that little altar of incense that somehow is as close as most of the priests can get to the Most Holy Place, and we think means prayer. Somehow I remember Betsalel telling us that you said the manna was a symbol that showed us that we don't live just by food, but by the words God speaks to us, is that right?"[25]

Moses nodded.

"So the second apartment is about discovering God's goodness, like the harvest festival, and being made good by him. Finally, I got thinking about that mystical Most Holy Place, with the special box and its golden cherubim. That's something like God's throne room, right? But maybe what's inside that box is very important, you know, the stone tablets with the rules. The only reason I can think of for having a set of rules is when you are deciding if someone has done the right thing or not. So I think maybe the last group of feasts, the trumpets and Yom Kippur and then the

24. Numb. 9:1–5
25. Deut 8:3

fun time with the feast of tabernacles, must be when God finally sorts everything out, decides who has given his load of wickedness to God, so God can decide who he can really pardon, like you begged God to do, right?"

Only the sound of a desert lark warbling in the terebinth foliage above them broke the utter silence following Jeriel's speech.

After what seemed an hour, when no one moved, Moses raised his face and beamed the most seraphic, radiant smile. "That's about it," he whispered. "You're absolutely right, my lad!"

Then, regaining his composure, he said, "Everything about the sanctuary shows us the steps in God's plan to bring us back completely to him, after the terrible mistake made in the garden. I hope you all know that tragic story from my first scroll?"[26] He smiled when most of his audience nodded vigorously. "Well now, there's one more thing I'd like to add today. When you roll your burdens of sin on to God you can't stop there. You have to let him take over, to change you so you become a new person, a good person. Now Betsalel, right here beside me, he's a wonderful example. God filled him with his Spirit, and this enabled him to build the sanctuary, and supervise others to help him build it."

"I thought he trained in all those crafts while he was in Egypt," observed one of the young men in Abitub and Elpaal's group. "I mean, to do what he did he'd have to have incredibly good training."

Before Moses could answer, Betsalel responded quickly. "Ahiram, without God none of us can do anything worthwhile that will last. True, I was offered some training in metallurgy and crafting while I was in Egypt, but I had nowhere near the adequate preparation needed to make the tabernacle. But when God's Spirit took over my life, he illuminated my mind, and I could do all the things he wanted me to do, even though I felt inadequate."

"That's absolutely true," interjected Oholiab. "Betsalel and I often used to talk about how amazing it was that God actually used us to make the sanctuary for him. Betsalel is a calm person, I'm a bit impetuous at times, but we made a wonderful team. It was the most amazing experience to let God take control."

"Same as me," said Moses laughing. "only Betsalel and Oholiab agreed to do what God asked them as soon as I approached them. But me, I refused God seven times before I finally realized that he would give me the power to do it!"

26. That is, Genesis chapter 3.

"You refused *God*?" said Jeriel in utter astonishment.

"I'm very ashamed to say that I did. Which just shows you what a wonderful, merciful, loving God we are following!"

There was considerable chatting as the group digested the incredible fact that the great man Moses had actually once refused to do what God asked. Most concluded God must be very patient, and were encouraged to commit themselves to him. Then a small boy in the front row, conspicuous by a severely crippled leg, asked, "Please Moses, does God have to carry our load forever, and ever, and ever?"

"That's a wonderful question son!" beamed Moses. "Now that lad there," pointing to Jeriel, and Betsalel whispered his name, "ah yes, Jeriel, has given a very important clue. He talked about the third Most Holy apartment and judgment, and that's what the special celebration of the Day of Atonement is all about."

"But that festival is very scary," observed a serious young woman. "It doesn't fix up anything for me! Wasn't it simply remembering what could happen to a person if they made God angry, like what happened to those young priests, Nadab and Abihu? They made just one silly mistake, and zrrrrip! God strikes them dead! That sounds like a pretty mean and angry God to me!"

"It's only scary if you think God is judging you, and if you haven't given him your load of sin to carry. What the Day of Atonement is really judging is the cause of sin, and shifting the load on to that cause."

Everyone, even Betsalel, looked puzzled.

"Let me try to explain," said Moses. "Betsalel tells me that you all have a good understanding about what a sin offering and a burnt offering means, right?" Most nodded vigorously. "Now on the day of Atonement there are five animals involved. There's a bull for a sin offering for the high priest—I presume you know there are different sin offerings for different people?" Again more nodding. "Then there are two rams for burnt offerings, one for all the people and one for the high priest as an ordinary person. And now we come to the goats." Suddenly everyone straightened up and was all attention. Those goats —that was the big question. What *did* they mean?

"Yes, the goats. The high priest casts lots between them. Casting lots is a way of saying the priest will allow God to choose, or if you like, judge. One of those goats is offered as a sin offering for all the people. It symbolically takes the load of sin that people are giving to God, just as we have spoken about. But the other goat does not give itself for anything. Nor does it receive any life-giving blood on itself. First the blood of the bull, then of the goat sin offering, are taken into God's presence in the Most Holy Place, with the priest burning clouds of incense so he will be protected from the glory of God. The high priest sprinkles blood from the sin offerings, first on the ark of the covenant, then the altar of incense, and then out in the courtyard on the bronze altar of burnt offering. Can you see he is spreading blood, the sign of life, from the most inside part of the tabernacle to the outside. It's like sweeping the load of sin from God's house right outside! Finally, with the load of sin swept completely out of God's house, the priest takes the last goat and presses *both* his hands on the head of it, and pronounces over it *all* the sins of the people. The priest uses three difference words to cover every possible type of sin: *awon*, meaning guilt and blame, all our tendencies to do wrong; *peshah*, which is just plain rebelliousness; and *chatta'ah* which is all those times we just don't get it right even when we try. By placing both hands on the head of the second goat the high priest indicates every sin, absolutely *every* sin, is dumped on the second goat, which is sent off to Azazel far, far away in the wilderness. Remember, all this is symbolic, to help us understand that God will finally not only judge evil as bad, but get rid of it completely."[27]

Moses scrutinized the blank faces in front of him. Jeriel tentatively raised his hand. "Are you saying that the scary Day of Atonement really means that the load of sin God is carrying for us is finally moved out of his house, and out of our camp, forever? That almost sounds as though it's God who's being judged, and not us! That's incredible, unbelievable! Although perhaps it's the goat that's sent away that's judged!"

Moses smiled. "That word Azazel is an odd one.[28] What we do know is all the sins are taken away, and don't come back. So someday, somehow, all the sins we load onto God will be entirely removed from, as you say, him, his house, and our camp."

Chelubai scratched his head, and Kenaz stroked his now flowing black beard. Everyone had faraway looks of deep concentration. "It sounds to me," suggested Kenaz thoughtfully, "that if we don't give God our loads of sin to carry we might end up carrying them ourselves out to that Azazel,

27. Lev 16:1–34

28. See Strong's concordance, *azazel* #5799, which suggests the word means "entire removal". It is variously translated as a place, or an evil angel, but the meaning remains elusive.

the entire removal place or person. I think I'll opt for God if you give me the choice!"

Betsalel ran his fingers through his hair, which, because of his work he liked to keep short, both it and his beard, and turned to Moses. "You know, this is the best thing I've heard in years. I've often felt very concerned that God was left carrying our load of guilt and suffering forever, but now that I know there is a final end in sight, I am deeply, deeply encouraged, and just so grateful. It sounds as though someday there will be no more need for sacrifices, but we will simply be God's friends forever."

Moses smiled happily. "That's how I understand it. We began today with the tragic molten calf story. The major problem at that time was people were not willing to wait for God. I have no idea when he will end all the sin and suffering we experience, but he will do it. Time for God is very different from what it is for us. We simply need to have confidence in him. Well, I hope you can all begin to see that the three apartments in the tabernacle, and the three festivals we enjoy and participate in, are all trying to teach us the stages of how we come closer to God, how he is in control and will work everything out so there is no more sin and suffering."

Chelubai was standing beside the group, leaning against the trunk of the terebinth tree. He straightened up, and raised his hand. "Moses, this is fascinating stuff. It's so good that God has woven into our ordinary yearly schedule ideas that help us understand his plans for us. But that goat in the desert is a puzzle. I've been out there in that burning heat often, and what always bothers me out there is the snakes. It's amazing that we don't have any in the camp. God must be actively protecting us. Anyway, that poor goat is likely to be attacked by those mean reptiles. Do you think that might have something to do with telling us that ultimately the snake that caused so much trouble in the garden for the first humans (which we know is really the Rebellious One who turned against God) will ultimately have to carry the burden and blame for all our mistakes?"

Moses looked pensive, and then slowly nodded. "That's an interesting thought, and I think you're right. Ultimately everything that has caused sin and suffering will be destroyed, forever. God carries our load of sin and suffering now, but eventually it will be dumped on the cause of it all."

"That's a very helpful idea," nodded Betsalel. "It makes sense." A murmur of voices indicated the idea was being discussed by others.

Suddenly a hand shot up. "Hey, Moses, all that sounds good, but you haven't told us about that last feast, *succoth*, the tabernacles one. It comes very soon after the scary Day of Atonement, doesn't it? I think it's only five days later, right? Can you help us with that, please?"[29] Obadiah had not lost his curiosity, even though he was now a man.

"Good question, Obadiah," responded Moses. "Thank you for reminding me. Now, I have to confess I have puzzled about the meaning of this feast. God specifically told me it was to remind us of how he brought us out of Egypt and we lived in booths here in the wilderness."[30]

A young boy in the middle of the group raised his hand, and waved it urgently. "Please, Moses, if it's to remind us of something, doesn't that mean the something has gone, that it's finished? Don't we all want to go to where we don't have to live in booths anymore, and have real homes that last forever and ever?"

"You're absolutely right, son," smiled Moses. "One of the very special things about this feast is that we're told it's a time for rejoicing,[31] and we're to make these little huts from the branches of lovely trees, different types of trees, which are not exactly plentiful out here in the desert. Remember there were lots of trees in the garden God made for the first couple.[32] So I think it is meant to be a picture of the ideal place, the first garden, with God in the center, and us all around him, with joy and peace and plenty because all evil has been taken away. It means we will be living with God, forever, without any sin or evil in the camp."

"I hope that's what it's going to be like when we get to the Promised Land," commented Joel.

"I do too, son," said Moses.

Everyone sat quietly and thoughtfully, pondering this amazing idea.

Then Abitub rose to his feet. "This has been an amazing time. Thank you so much, both of you, Betsalel and Moses," he said, and a great chorus of amens[33] rose from the group.

29. Lev. 23:26–43
30. Lev 23:42–43
31. Lev 23:40
32. Gen. 2:9
33. "Amen" is Hebrew for "truly".

11

Battering Fire and Love

The years of wandering were coming to an end. There was a general air of optimism in the camp, as Moses constantly reassured everyone that God meant what he said, and the forty years of wandering were almost over.

Betsalel now did very little repair work for the Israelite camp. True to his calling as a teacher, he had trained a team of reliable and capable people, led by Chelubai and Jahath, to take over from him and Oholiab both the construction of utensils and tools, and the mending and restoration work.

To his immense sorrow Oholiab had died just a few weeks earlier. The death was swift and Oholiab suffered little, but Betsalel deeply mourned his friend. They had shared so much together, so many memories. As he and the original "gang" (Phinehas, Assir, Joel, Jahath, Kenaz, Obadiah, Chelubai, Mishael, Abitub, Elpaal and Mikael) slowly walked from the grave, he felt his own life must soon end. He was the very last of the over-twenty-year-olds at the time of the rebellion at Kadesh Barnea to still be alive. Only Moses, Joshua, Caleb, and Eleazar were still alive.[1] Wrapped in grief tinted with self-pity, he hardly noticed Kenaz tugging at his *kutōnet*, and when he finally did, he answered rather gruffly, "Yes?"

"Listen," urged Kenaz. "Can you hear the oriole singing? It's up there on that little branch with the three leaves at the end. I'll never forget when I first saw an oriole, on our first trip down the Brook of Egypt."

---

1. Eleazar must have been over 30 at the time of the rebellion, because he was already an anointed priest. It appears he was the one person not mentioned by name who was exempt from the death decree.

Betsalel almost unwillingly glanced into the terebinth tree, and there was the golden bird pouring forth its song in symphonic radiance. He nodded faintly and smiled weakly, but memories of many bird expeditions and countless other times with the young man walking beside him flooded his heart. As he trudged back to camp he realized what a blessing the group had been to him, and what he had originally thought was a service to them, had returned as a sevenfold benefit on his own head.

"That bird will always remind me of you," said Kenaz softly. "How can I ever thank you for all you've done to share God's love with us?" Wordlessly, Betsalel patted his companion's shoulder.

But there was one small duty Betsalel had been procrastinating over for days, and the longer he left it, the worse he felt about his neglect, and the less able to do it. He should go and visit Moses, but he couldn't think of the words to say to his old friend.

Yes, the great news was the days of wandering were indeed almost over. Going round and round in circles in the wilderness, even if sheltered by the cloud when it was hot, and warmed by its fire when they were cold, had too often felt utterly aimless. But now they were moving north. They were nearly there! Yet things had not been easy for Moses, and there were signs he was struggling to cope.

First, his sister Miriam had died.[2] Betsalel realized this was very emotional for Moses because of the vital role his sister had played in his survival as a baby.[3] Of course he did not remember as she watched his bitumen-covered little basket floating on the River Nile, nor how she engaged the formidable Princess in conversation, winning the right for their own mother to care for him! What incredible courage Miriam had shown. But Moses had heard the story many times from both his mother and sister, and could live every moment of it. There was no official mourning for Miriam, for she was only a woman, even if a very good one. But Betsalel felt sad, and thought there should have been some special recognition given for this remarkable person.

Then before Moses could recover from his grief, the water supply that had followed them all their forty years of wandering dried up. The people, remembering nothing, began cursing and clamoring for drastic action. Moses and Aaron, now very old men, went to God's tabernacle to gain

2. Num. 20:1
3. Exod. 2:1–9

wisdom, and God did not fail them. "Go to the rock," they were told, "and *tell* the rock to give its water."[4]

Moses obeyed—almost. In frustrated exhaustion he yelled "Hear you rebels! Shall we bring water for you out of this rock?" Then he hit it with his rod, twice for good measure.[5] It was so logical, exactly what he had done forty years before in virtually the same situation. And it worked, miraculously, both times! Water gushed from the battered rock.

But it wasn't what God requested; the consequences were swift. Hitting the rock to get water was cliché. God had planned something new, something utterly unexpected: merely speaking to the rock would inexplicably, miraculously produce water. God would thus be signally honored, and not Moses' technical expertise. For this apparent tiny failure God announced that Moses, Moses of all people, was forbidden to enter the Promised Land![6] The people were truly contrite when they realized what their grumbling had caused, but they could not undo their mistake, or its effects on Moses.

Then Moses had another shock. A very polite request to the Edomites to allow Israel to walk through their land using the Kings Highway, the main international road that any traveler was allowed to use on their way north from Egypt to Elam, was arrogantly, viciously, refused. A large, hostile army of Edomites greeted them, and the Israelites were forced to trudge slowly, painfully, and complainingly, through the eastern desert conditions.[7]

Then came the final blow — on this slow and dreary detoured journey, Aaron died. At Mount Hor, on the edge of inhospitable Edom, God told the brothers it was now time for Aaron to perish. A sad trio climbed the mountain, and at the top Moses stripped his brother of his magnificent high priestly robes, invested them on Aaron's son Eleazar (father of Phineas), and buried his brother. This time the whole camp supported Moses in his grief with thirty days of heart-felt mourning.[8]

At this discouraging time God even gave the people, and perhaps especially Moses, a tiny taste of what he had promised, conquest of the

4. Numb. 20:2–9

5. Numb. 20:10–11

6. Numb 20:12–13, cf. Exod. 17:1–7.)

7. Numb.20:14–21.

8. Numb. 20:22–29

promised land. When attacked by the vicious king of Arad, from southern Canaan, God granted them total victory over him and his hordes.[9]

But although the people's mourning for Aaron was genuine, and no doubt their gratitude for victory was real, their memories remained short, with more grumbling about food and water. This caused God to cease protection and allow poisonous serpents (from whom they had miraculously been protected in all their wanderings) to invade the camp in large numbers. From Betsalel's point of view, things were getting about as bad as when they had rebelled at Kadesh Barnea decades earlier. Finally, worse, Moses himself seemed to have lost his bearings. Incredibly, he made a bronze serpent, put it on a pole, and told the people to look at it and they would live! It seemed the horror of the golden calf was again overwhelming them, even Moses![10]

Betsalel leaned heavily on his staff as he made his way with dogged determination to Moses' tent. It was not a great distance, because they both lived on the eastern side of the tabernacle. He did not feel old, but was aware that over the last few weeks the aging process had accelerated in his body. Confronting Moses filled him with dread.

Betsalel was a little surprised to discover Moses seated in his tent at a small table, busy writing. But at least it gave an easy opening gambit. "Good morning, old friend," he called to Moses from the doorway of the tent. "Still writing laws?"

Moses looked up, and smiled broadly. "Come in my young friend! I'm writing a speech, the one I plan to deliver to the people as my last testament."

Betsalel gulped. Not only had Moses called him young, but he seemed completely content, no sign of grief and resentment against God for denying him entry into Canaan. "Aren't—aren't you sad about not going to Canaan?"

Moses' gaze never wavered. "Son, you've been living with that sentence for forty years, same as I have. Are you angry with Yahweh?"

"N-no, at least, not much," admitted Betsalel. "But it did take me a long time to get used to it. The news of the forty years' wandering was followed by that terrible Korah, Dathan, and Abiram revolt, and the horror of that and the punishments that followed took me months to get over. Months, maybe years."

9. Numb. 21:1–3
10. Numb. 21:4–9.

"Me too," smiled Moses. "No one seemed to notice that when the people rebelled there at Kadesh Barnea Yahweh said *nobody* over twenty years of age, except Caleb and Joshua, would enter Canaan.[11] Yes, I made a dreadful mistake there at Meribah when I hit that rock. I completely ruined an amazing picture of the goodness of God. But God knows I'm truly, truly sorry. And I also know these people absolutely must have another leader, or they will worship me as their god. Joshua is a good man, a great soldier, and has been my helper for many years. I know God will support him as he leads the people through the wars they must encounter to take possession of the land. I had a bit of experience with war when I was a prince in Egypt, but it wasn't for me.[12] But Joshua is a natural, as you'll remember when he led the battle with the Amalekites. He's God's man to conquer Canaan. By the way, remember his real name is Hoshea, meaning rescue, but I changed it to Joshua, *Yahweh* rescues. I wanted both he and the people to recognize that it is only Yahweh who rescues us, not any mere mortal. Remember the battle we won against the Amalekites was only when I raised my hands in prayer to God. It was an incredible experience. Joshua is a very important name."[13]

"You astound me," said Betsalel. "Virtually everyone I know worships God to get something from him, to get all the blessings he offers, but you seem to be utterly content to simply have him as your friend."[14]

"You've got it, Betsalel! Being God's friend is the most important blessing anyone can ever have!" Moses smiled triumphantly. "And you know, that land of Canaan is not the ultimate goal. When Yahweh showed me the pattern of the sanctuary, he also revealed the ultimate plan is renewal of this whole earth now so messed up by sin and suffering. An earth made new, that's the true Promised Land, my hope, my dream."

"You told me that when you gave me the tabernacle plans," smiled Betsalel. "Actually, that's what helped me cope with my own sentence of banishment from the Promised Land Canaan over that river Jordan. It's a bit indistinct, a hazy idea, that true Promised Land idea, but I trust God."

Moses closed his eyes in meditation, and his uplifted face glowed with the same inner glory that had lighted it when he came back from the

11. Numb. 14:20–35

12. *Josephus,* p57–58

13. Exod. 17:8–16; Numb. 13:16. Joshua is Hebrew, Jesus is simply the Greek version of the same name.

14. Exod. 33:11

mountain with the second tables of stone written on by God.[15] A deep and utter peace enveloped both men, but finally Moses opened his eyes and said, "Son, there's something on your mind. What is it?"

Betsalel coughed, spluttered, cleared his throat. And Moses smiled, waiting patiently. Finally, Betsalel gave up all pretense and blurted out, "Why did you make an idol?"

And Moses threw back his head and laughed, laughed with abandoned delight. "Simply because Yahweh told me to!"[16] He laughed so much he lost his breath.

"What!"

"Son," said Moses gently, when he had regained his composure, "you had a wonderful vision of teaching young people the truth about the sanctuary and its services. I thank God for that, every day. But you know, there are many out there who have not been willing to learn from you, nor from those you taught. So we have a problem. Instead of understanding that the sanctuary and its services are symbolic of something beyond our understanding, something that Yahweh has still to do for us, I've discovered there are many who think those services and sacrifices give them merit with God; that instead of giving the load of sin to God, they think they can be good for God by their own efforts, by offering enough sacrifices. Now, here in this speech I'm writing out for them to keep forever, I've tried to talk about this issue. Let me find it." Moses ran his fingers along the densely written Hebrew characters, peering with squinting eyes.[17] "Ah, here it is: 'Circumcise therefore the foreskin of your heart, and be no longer stubborn.'[18] That should get them thinking! I mean, who can do that for themselves? Who can circumcise themselves in the ordinary way, let alone their own hearts? They must recognize that real circumcision is something that is done for them by Yahweh himself!"

"But Moses!" interrupted Betsalel, scratching his head in bewilderment. "Surely you know that the young ones, and that means virtually all the people now, have *not* been circumcised! Everyone who came out of

15. Exod. 34:29–35

16. Numb. 21:8

17. Classic Hebrew was written without paragraphs, sentences, or even gaps between the words. This may seem impossible to us, but it had one big advantage: people were forced to read whole passages, and not merely pick and choose verses they liked!

18. Deut. 10:16

Egypt was circumcised, but no one born in the wilderness wandering has been."[19]

"I suppose you think I've been negligent?" Moses smiled, and Betsalel gave a faint, embarrassed nod of agreement. "But Yahweh told me to wait, wait till circumcision would really mean something to them. I well remember the trouble I got into because I neglected to circumcise my own son.[20] So I know how important it is. But the people need to know that circumcision is not just a rite, it is deeply symbolic of our commitment to God. It is the sign of the covenant El Shaddai renewed with Abraham, after he made the terrible mistake with Hagar.[21] When the people cross that Jordon River, that will be the time for them to all discover that belonging to God is not an easy option. I pray they will be ready. Look, at the end of my speech I've reminded them again of what circumcision means." Again Moses ran his finger along the long lines of carefully inscribed letters. "Ah, here it is! 'And the LORD your God will circumcise your heart and the heart of your offspring, so that you will love the LORD your God with all your heart and with all your soul, that you may live.'"[22]

"Hmm, I'm learning every day!" Betsalel cleared his throat and took another deep breath. How do you tell someone like Moses he has done something wrong? "But Moses, shouldn't we keep the people from idolatry?"

"A very important question. At the bottom of the mountain, that mountain of fire, the people thought they could do everything God wanted all by themselves, 'All that the Lord has said, we will do,' they said, three times.[23] So God allowed that terrible mistake with the molten calf to show them what they really needed was for him to carry the load of their guilt."

"B-b-but," stammered Betsalel, "why a bronze snake idol? And you made it for them! Surely it doesn't make any difference what metal it was made of?" With horror, Betsalel saw Moses' eyes twinkle, and he almost expected him to laugh again.

"No it doesn't matter about metals. Gold, or bronze, they're all the same to Yahweh. But did you notice there was no ceremony with that bronze serpent? The people just had to look, and they'd live. That's called

19. Josh 5:2–9

20. Exod. 4:24–26

21. See Gen chapter 17. The original covenant with Abraham was made before the Hagar incident, in Gen chapter 15.

22. Deut. 30:6

23. Exod. 19:8, 24:3,7

having faith. I know they can turn it into magic, but I pray they will understand God's message. It's the very message I spoilt, ruined, when I hit the rock instead of speaking to it. And someday, Yahweh showed me, Yahweh himself will come and be lifted up before the people, and they must choose whether they believe him, or not. When God is first lifted up, for some people he will merely look like a snake. He won't seem good or special at all. But they must trust him."[24]

This was a great deal for Betsalel to digest. He sat thoughtfully bowed in prayer, his chin cupped in his hands.

Moses interrupted him. "Now I must tell you an amazing story, one that will surely bolster your faith in God and bring joy to your heart. No one can fail to see that our people are camped in the plains of Moab, on the east of the Jordan River, and after the recent and very successful skirmishes we've had with the local tribes, that King of Arad, and then Sihon King of the Amorites,[25] other communities have good reason to be scared. Now, as you know I do have contacts with many local people, and old friends often visit me. Last week I had such a visit, and what a story he shared!"[26]

"Perhaps God sent you out into the wilderness so you'd have friends while we all wandered here," laughed Betsalel.

"Maybe," grinned Moses. "We all know God told us to leave Moab and Ammon alone, but they are frightened stupid. So the Moabite King Balak sent for an old renegade prophet living up in the north, a man called Balaam. The idea was King Balak would heavily reimburse—I'd call it bribe —Balaam if he would come down and magically curse our people, and thus remove the threat we pose to their nation. This Balaam has some idea of the true God, and he refused the offer, but the stakes were raised, and he persuaded 'God' to let him collect his reward.

"But now comes the delightful part of the story! On the way down to Moab this Balaam's donkey became very rebellious, and refused to obey orders. But when Balaam beat the poor animal it talked to him! Just wouldn't you love to hear a talking donkey? That mere donkey told him cursing Israel was wrong and it said it was protecting Balaam from an angel sent from God to destroy him! You'd think a talking ass would make Balaam turn round and go home as fast as that amazing donkey would carry him, but the lure of money and fame was too great. King Balak was very pleased

24. See John 3:14–15
25. Numb. 21:1–3, 21–35
26. See Numb. Chapters 22—24 for the following account.

to see Balaam, despite the warning straight from God that Balaam could only say what God allowed him to say. Balaam tried no less than four times to curse us, all after elaborate sacrificial ceremonies, but not once was he successful. King Balak was understandably very angry with these repeated failures, and Balaam missed out on his house full of gold and silver. Son, the message is getting out there that Yahweh is fighting for us, just like he did all those years ago on the banks of the Red Sea."[27]

"That's an incredible story," agreed Betsalel, shaking his head in wonder. "A talking donkey! Are you sure it's true? Do you trust the person who told you? Are you going to put it in your book?"

"I'm absolutely sure it's true, and yes I will most definitely include it in the fourth book. But son, there's something that's worrying me. Balaam might not have been able to curse us, but I see many of our people are getting far too friendly with our Moabite and Midianite neighbors, many of whom don't worship our Creator God of heaven. Keep your eyes open, and you'll see that there's a lot more so-called 'trading' going on than there was previously. I fear what Balaam could not achieve by cursing he may accomplish by inappropriate social connections. There are a number of very attractive foreign women wandering around our camp these days."

"Surely the people wouldn't be so foolish!"

"I'm afraid I don't trust them. They show every sign of making all the same terrible mistakes their parents did. They've already complained about food and water,[28] and we just need these foreigners to encourage the people to lose all restraint[29] as they did with that calf, and we're back in exactly the same tragic situation."

"Oh, Moses! Surely they won't go that far! Not all that awful sex orgy and dancing to that useless creature! Not after what they know happened to their fathers! Surely not!"

"I hope not, but I fear the worst."

Betsalel shook his head sadly, lost in thought.

"My beloved son, there'll always be some who go their own way, but remember God is with us. That story about Balaam and his donkey brings joy to my heart. If Yahweh can control a donkey's speech, and an old renegade's utterances, he can still keep us safe. Let me show you a little taste of what I wanted to show you when you came in. This speech of mine. I'm still working on it, see here: I jot down ideas on this damaged piece of

27. Exod. 14:14
28. Numb. 20:3–5 cf. Exod. 15:22—16:3
29. Exod. 32:25

parchment." Moses pulled a few scraps of parchment towards himself, put one aside, then looked at the others.

"Ah, yes, right near the start I'll tell them about my failure at Meribah, and their failures too. I hope that will make them listen. But what I really want to do is show them what God is like. They weren't there to see the fire, so I tell them over, and over again about that incredible *ha-esh*, the luminous majesty. I planned to put it in fourteen times, but I think it has sneaked in a bit more![30] Yes, our God is a consuming fire.[31] But what I really want them to see is the incredible love of God. I've put that in fourteen times, after the molten calf story!"[32]

"I've always thought of God as caring for us, but not exactly as loving us," responded Betsalel thoughtfully.

"Because God loves us, he wants our love in return. And so I'll share with you a passage in my speech that makes my soul shout for joy. '*Hear Oh, Israel! The Lord our God, the Lord is one! You shall love the Lord thy God with all your heart, and with all your soul and with all your might.*'[33] Now tell me, does that sound like a command, a plea, or maybe even a love proposal?"

"A plea," whispered Betsalel. "certainly a deep desire for love."

"Yes, exactly. And to think that I battered the symbol of that glorious God of love with my stupid rod!" Tears rolled down Moses' face.[34]

Betsalel waited until Moses calmed, and then said, "I think you've answered all my questions."

"Great, but I discovered something. In my first scroll, "Beginnings," the first time I used the word love, *aheb*, is when God tested Abraham and asked him to sacrifice Isaac, the son he dearly loved.[35] You know, Yahweh did not ask Abraham to stop loving Isaac. But God did want to know who Abraham loved most. How I wish I could help people understand it is our love that God wants, and good behavior is only the result of that love! When we truly love him God gives us all that's worthwhile and precious!"

---

30. Deut. 4:11, 12, 15, 33, 36 x2, 5:4, 5, 22, 23, 24, 25, 26, 9;10,10:4. The word fire occurs many times throughout the book of Deuteronomy.

31. Deut. 4:24 cf. Heb.12:29.

32. Deut. 6:4, 7:7, 8, 9x2,12, 13, 10:12, 15, 18, 19, 11;1, 13, 22.

33. Deut. 6:4

34. That Moses was an emotional person can be seen in his responses to the unjust taskmaster, throwing the first tables of stone when he saw the rebellion of the Israelites at Sinai, and then hitting the rock. Thus it is not inappropriate to portray him as weeping.

35. Gen 22:2

You Shall Love the Lord.

"You've just answered something that has bothered me for a long time," mused Betsalel thoughtfully. "I've never doubted the goodness of God, and that what he does is right. But sometimes I've puzzled why he destroys people, like, well, like Korah, Dathan, and Abiram. It seems he can forgive and cope with so many of our mistakes, but now I understand that if we really, truly don't love him, then there can be no relationship with him, just eternal misery on both sides. We have to part company, and parting company with God means losing the source of life."

"Yes, that's exactly what I've come to understand. It gives me much joy to hear that you understand too!" Moses wiped his eyes, and gazed into the distance.

"And now I would like to share something with you. Somehow I thought it was a bit too personal to put in the speech. It's really a prayer, but it fits both you and me, and I wrote you a copy on one of these fragments of parchment. Yes, it's a prayer, a heart cry from an old man. I think you'll understand." Moses passed a scrap of vellum to Betsalel, who read:

A PRAYER OF MOSES, THE MAN OF GOD

Lord, you have been our dwelling place in all generations
before the mountains were brought forth
or ever you had formed the earth and the world
from everlasting to everlasting, you are God.

You return man to dust,
and say, "Return O children of man!"
For a thousand years in your sight
are but as yesterday when it is past,
or as a watch in the night.

You sweep them away as with a flood; they are like a dream,
like grass that is renewed in the morning;
in the morning it flourishes and is renewed,
in the evening it fades and withers.

For we are brought to an end by your anger;
by your wrath we are dismayed.
You have set our iniquities before you,
our secret sins in the light of your presence.

For all our days pass away under your wrath;
  we bring our years to an end like a sigh.
The years of our lives are seventy,
  or even by strength eighty,
    yet their span is but toil and trouble:
    they are soon gone and we fly away.
Who considers the power of your anger,
  and your wrath, according to the fear of you?

So teach us to number our days
  that we may get a heart of wisdom. Return, O LORD! How long?
Have pity on your servants!
Satisfy us in the morning with your steadfast love,
  that we may rejoice and be glad all our days.
Make us glad for as many days as you have afflicted us,
  and for as many years as we have seen evil.
Let your work be shown to your servant,
  and your glorious power to their children.

Let the favor of the Lord our God be upon us,
  and establish the work of our hands upon us,
Yes, establish the work of our hands! (Psalm 90, ESV)

"Oh, Moses!" exclaimed Betsalel, "I understand so well. Especially that last appeal: establish the work of our hands. I know that nothing I've done has been without the power of God working through me, but I fear it will be destroyed by others."

"Yes, that's exactly what I fear," said Moses. "Destroyed, or misunderstood."

"I guess we must give it all to God," suggested Betsalel, and Moses smiled.

"That's exactly what I meant in my prayer!" Moses agreed, adding, "I might have answered your questions, or at least some of them, but let's meet again, tomorrow, or very soon. To talk about God's love!"

12

Mere Statistics

Moses' prayer filled Betsalel with wonder. To think that Moses, the friend of God, was haunted by exactly the same doubts and worries that bothered him was strangely comforting. Finally, Betsalel realized it wasn't the desire to produce something eternal that was the issue, but simply whether God could bless what he had done. Despite his fears, the tabernacle had not only survived its forty years of wilderness weather, but was truly as good as new. It would be very safe to leave in God's hands, to trust whatever God planned for it. And Betsalel was sure the endless effort Moses had expended, not only in governing the people, but also in meticulously writing out all that had happened to them, and all that God had spoken to him, could be safely left in God's care as well. Leaving something for posterity had been a big concern for Egyptian leaders, but if a person trusted God, he need have no worries. Everything would work out according to God's plan, and that was all that mattered.

The picture of God being both fire and love inspired Betsalel's meditations. The more he pondered the idea, the more he realized its truth. He remembered the love he'd had for his own delightful young wife, a love cut short so tragically.[1] It was during the plague of locusts, when the days of suffering were almost over. His wife, a virtuous woman, had insisted she return some cooking pots she had borrowed from a friendly Egyptian neighbor. The neighbor was not only friendly, but decent and true, but on the way home Betsalel's wife was accosted by three drunken slave taskmasters

---

1. The story of Betsalel's wife is pure conjecture, but not implausible, see for example, Judges chapter 19, and remembering the Israelites were slaves without right of choice.

who repeatedly abused her in every possible way. His wife struggled home, humiliated and bleeding copiously, but despite his best efforts to save her, she died in his arms. As he pondered Moses prayer he realized his wife's terrible tragedy had galvanized his decision to abandon the allurements of the Egyptians, and follow the people of God in their quest for freedom. She was thus a blessing to him even in her tragic death, and he never stopped loving her with a pure and holy fire. As he had indicated to young Joel, it had taken time, and pain, to realize that loving his wife was different from the love he had for his siblings and mates. But all effort to discover who she really was, and appreciate her contribution to his life, were amply rewarded. It was like learning to know God more.

For years Betsalel had shared, and loved, the idea that the tabernacle services showed how God carries our burden of sin and suffering. But as he thought of his wife, he realized truly loving God may mean not only the desire to be a friend of God, and but also a willingness to share the burden of carrying the problems of others. How many times had he wished he could have taken the wounds his wife so undeservingly received from those brutish men! He knew Moses was God's special friend, and was shocked by Moses' quiet acceptance of God's refusal to let him enter the Promised Land. Moses loved God just for God himself, and not for anything that God did for him. Surely that was what Moses was trying to say in the passage he had so affectionately read out, the passage about loving God with everything a person had.

A few days after their discussion, Betsalel returned to Moses' tent, not with anything to tell or ask, but just to see if Moses had something he wanted to talk about regarding his friend God. Once again he found Moses busy writing. "Still working on the speech?" he asked, teasingly.

"Yes, I really want to help these people see Yahweh." Moses paused, laid down his brush, and put the lid on his ink pot. "I realize I'm going to go down in history as the lawmaker. I don't mind that. Laws are important. They are the foundation of any healthy society. They reveal the character of those who make them. Good laws come from good people, and of course, God's laws are perfect.

"But law is not enough. Think of a marriage based on laws, just a contract. It wouldn't be much fun, would it? I've put all the laws into this speech, but I've added (with God's permission) a few little extras to show that it's more than just law, to remind the people that they are to love Yahweh, not just obey him.[2] How do you like this idea? When a man marries he should not go to war for a whole year so he can spend happy times with his wife.[3] That rule should definitely show everyone that love is important! And this one: when a person sees their friend or neighbor's donkey wandering away they should return it to the rightful owner; or if the donkey has fallen under their load, they should help the neighbor and his donkey.[4] Little things like this are more than just law. They should help people see that what they are supposed to do is love their neighbors. I know I've told them that before,[5] but I'm trying to do it in many different ways so they will understand. I've told them about cities of refuge, where people who commit crimes unwittingly can flee, and I've told them about the importance of having at least two witnesses to a crime, and even more important, that they must never, ever, bear false witness. A false witness is absolutely opposite God's ways, and should be treated as he intended others to be treated. I just hope they understand it's the false witnesses that are to receive an eye for an eye, a tooth for a tooth, or hand for hand.[6] That eye for eye stuff does sound harsh, but they must understand it only applies to terrible situations like false witnesses. I hope they understand this is all about treating other people in the way we would like to be treated ourselves."

Betsalel smiled. "That's a great guide: treat people the way you'd like to be treated yourself. I love it!"

"Yes, I've spent a great deal of time thinking about what really makes keeping a law a loving action, not merely a duty. Dutiful obedience avoids consequences, so I've tried to talk about those. I've included a long list of curses, you know, all those bad outcomes no one wants, that result from disobedience.[7] I mean it's all pretty obvious, but I've tried to write it out so that even the most simple minded can understand. And I've balanced it with a splendid list of blessings that can result from obeying, and that God wants his people to worship him with joyfulness and gladness.[8] Look, I've told them plainly that what counts is obeying Yahweh joyfully, and in gladness of heart.

2. See, for example, Deut. 19:9

3. Deut 24:5

4. Deut 22:1–4

5. Lev 19:18

6. Deut 19:1–21

7. Deut 27: 9–26, 28:15–46

8. Deut 28:1–14, 47

"So yes, I've tried to get to the essence of what makes obeying a joyful experience, not mere drudgery. I realized when people *allow* God to circumcise their hearts, then they will *love* him.[9] So, what's my final conclusion? It's simply a matter of loving choice. And of course, choice is a personal decision. I hope no one misses this point about choice and joyfulness: '*This commandment is not too hard. It's not in heaven that you need to go up there; it's not over the sea that you have to travel for it. No, it's very near you, in your heart, so that you can do it'*. Of course, it means a person must choose, in their own heart. God has never forced anyone. Who did he force to leave Egypt? No one. Everyone was so keen to go! He has clearly given us options. So that's what I will say. '*I call heaven and earth to witness against you today, that I have set before you life and death, blessing and curse. Therefore, choose life, that you and your offspring may live, loving the lord your God, obeying his voice and holding fast to him, for he is your life and length of days*'.[10]"

"That makes things pretty clear," smiled Betsalel admiringly.

"And I'll present Joshua to them, endorsing him as my successor. I'll need to remind both him and them that it's God who is their true leader, the one who will fight their battles for them."[11]

"You've just answered something I've been mulling in my mind since our last talk together," responded Betsalel. "I too have been wondering, what is the critical factor in love? I'm sure you're right when you identify it as choice."

Moses nodded. "Exactly," he said. "Anyone can obey because they are forced to, when they are too scared not to, or even if they can see the advantages of obeying. But it's only when a person *chooses* to obey because they *love* the person making the rules, that obedience is really more than just compliance."

"You've set yourself quite a task with that speech," observed Betsalel. "I pray God will help the people understand what you've tried to tell them."

"I can only do my best, and leave it to God to do the rest. Yes, the key to keeping all these laws is choice and love."

"The problem is, so few people understand real love," remarked Betsalel.

Moses turned to his friend. "That's just it!" he exclaimed. "They think of it as a sensation, a momentary pleasure. How few recognize it as lifelong

9. Deut. 30:6

10. Deut. 30:11–20

11. Deut 31:7–8

commitment, of giving everything for someone." Moses was quiet for a few moments, and then added. "As well as the speech, I want to share a song with the people. Music somehow cements things into the mind. Of course, I made a terrible mistake at that rock, hitting it instead of speaking in love. So the theme of my song is about who is our true Rock."

Moses pulled another scrap of parchment towards himself, saying, "This is just some of what I've written, but you'll get the idea. 'For I will proclaim the name of the Lord; ascribe greatness to our God! The Rock, his work is perfect, for all his ways are justice. A God of faithfulness and without iniquity.'[12]"

"That makes it very clear," observed Betsalel. "Beautiful."

"I hope so," responded the old man, "but I know what will happen. The people will keep on rebelling and doing things in their own way. So what do you think of this part, 'But Jeshurun[13] grew fat, and kicked; you grew fat, stout, and sleek; then he forsook the God who made him and scoffed at the Rock of his salvation.' And this, 'You were unmindful of the Rock that bore you, you forgot the God who gave you birth.'"[14]

Moses paused, and gazed through his tent door. "Yes, I'm afraid people love the tangible, rather than the eternal. See those young women over there? Possibly nice girls, but they don't know God, and are enticing our people to visit their shrines. That horrible forgetfulness is already happening. I better call an assembly at the tabernacle, and try to warn them." Moses got up, and went to do his duty.

Elders and heralds quickly responded to Moses' summons, and people gathered at the appointed place at the front of the tabernacle. As he explained what would happen if they were unfaithful to Yahweh, and urged them to remain true to their God because they were on the very borders of the Promised Land, many began weeping. They knew he was telling the truth, for many had friends and family who had been meeting with the friendly, seductive ambassadresses.

At that moment a breathless Phinehas burst into the assembly. "Moses!" he gasped. "You were right! People have been going off with those Midianites and doing all sorts of shocking things at their worship places. And now a terrible sickness is raging through the camp, especially in the

---

12. Deut 32:3–4

13. Jeshurun means "Upright one". It is a poetic name for Israel.

14. Deut 32:15, 18

southern part of it, in the camps of Reuben, Gad and Simeon. Why, look out there! Can you see them?"

People were running to the entrance of the tabernacle, weeping and praying, begging for the plague to stop. But while Phinehas was still speaking Zimri, chief of the Simeonites, brazenly walked through the camp fondly escorting a lavishly dressed, supremely confident woman called Cozbi, daughter of the leader of the local Midianites. She arrogantly carried a large replica of her god right past the tabernacle door!

Moses called. "Zimri! You are a leader of our people! Stand for truth, not licentiousness!"

Zimri turned, and smirking contemptuously at the great leader sneered, "Surely truth must be learned from many people! Who says you know all the truth about everything? Are you the only one God has spoken to? You're just old, with no idea how to enjoy life! Stop denying pleasure, excitement and true love to others! I will learn from those who know a great deal more of the world than you do!" He strode off purposefully, arm protectively around Cozbi.

The weeping crowd outside the tent, even Moses, at first appeared paralyzed by Zimri's brazen and shameless discourtesy. Then Moses, after fervently praying that God would reveal how he should deal with the matter, gave orders that anyone who had joined themselves to Baal Peor worship should be killed.[15] Phinehas stared at Moses, then at Zimri in horror. Then grabbing a spear from one of the tabernacle guards, he raced after the couple to their tent, and impaled them both.[16]

It was so quick, so harsh. Betsalel felt physically sick, and vomited. Where was this love for God now? Perhaps closer than he realized, for immediately Moses received the message from God he had been waiting for. The drastic action of Phinehas had stopped the plague, and God had given Phineas a special covenant of peace, as well as a perpetual priesthood.[17] But Betsalel returned to his tent a sad and troubled man.

A few days later Betsalel asked his family to move his bed out to the nearby grove of the terebinth trees he loved so well. They protested gently, but he insisted the weather was mild, and he wanted to have time to meditate and commune with God. His family were disturbed by his

15. Numb. 25:4–5

16. Numb. 25:1–18. See also Josephus, p82–93, which adds details (such as carrying the image) to the biblical story.

17. Numb. 25:10–13.

request, remembering one of the laws given by Moses. If a man died in a tent, everyone that came into that tent would be unclean. "His time must be near," they concluded, "and selfless to the end, he does not want to cause us any trouble."[18] Betsalel may have wanted to be alone to meditate, to spare his family from pollution, but there was always someone with him, asking for advice, offering words of comfort. In ones, twos, or threes, people came to the terebinth grove and visited him. Frequently they were from the first small group he had started so many years before. Then there were those who had learned reading and writing and the words of Moses from the groups the first group started, and then to his immense surprise, many others came, telling how they had learned the things of God and the words of Moses from one of his former students.

Soon after the disastrous plague involving Zimri and Cozbi God instructed Moses and Eleazar, who, after the death of his father Aaron, was now high priest, to conduct a census of all the men aged twenty years old and above.[19] This created a good deal of excitement among the people, because the last time a census had been taken was just before they left Sinai. Clearly this new census was in preparation for the conquest of Canaan. Now, after forty years of apparently aimless wandering, things were happening! Leaders from each tribe were appointed, and quickly did their duty. When all the calculations were made, the leaders gathered to give their reports to the leaders. Joshua was there, as new leader-elect, all the tribal leaders, and of course Moses and Eleazar, with the priests Phinehas and Ithamar.

For those camped to the north of the tabernacle the numbers were encouraging. Both the tribes of Dan and Asher had increased, from 62,700 to 64,400 and 41,500 to 53,400 respectively. But the tribe of Naphtali, well known for their love of good living, had decreased from 53,400 to 45,440. But overall there was an increase in population.

On the western camp there was also generally good news. Manasseh had increased dramatically from 32,200 to 52,700, and Benjamin, the least in Israel, from 35,400 to a very healthy 45,600. But sadly the tribe of Ephraim had decreased significantly from 40,500 to 32,500. This put a worried frown on Joshua's face, but he knew many of his own tribe had been all too friendly with the Midianites.

18. Numb. 19:14

19. Num 26:1-2

Eleazar shook his head mournfully. "I think, Moses, it must be the ravages from the plague contracted from that tragic Beth-Peor incident."[20] Moses nodded thoughtfully. "I think you're right."

As the numbers for the southern camp, those of Reuben, Simeon and Gad, were counted, Eleazar's observation was tragically, dramatically, endorsed. The tribe of Reuben had decreased from 46,500 to 43,730. The tribe of Gad had also fallen, from 45,650 to 40,500. But the tribe of Simeon, the one led by the defiant Zimri, had plummeted from 59,300 to just 22,200.

"That plague almost wiped out a whole tribe," said Eleazar miserably. "I'm almost afraid to count the last group! But think, that southern area was the part of the camp where Korah and his rebellion had the most impact! Seems that rebellion has cast a very long forty-year shadow of insurrection!"

"Grumbling always destroys the heart," observed Joshua. "I remember when I was a spy, those forty years ago, and the ten who gave the bad report began their grumbling right in the Promised land. We all make mistakes, but grumbling and murmuring destroys from the inside out. I'm sure those grumblers never meant to do the damage they did, but they simply would not listen to Caleb and me. They focused on the few, the very few, tall giants of Anak that we met."

"Take courage," said Moses. "The eastern camp is closest to the priests, those most loyal to God. Let's see what those numbers tell us. Apart from the devastation in Simeon, the numbers in the other tribes have been basically stable. But if something is different with these eastern tribes, we may be able to see the glory of God at work before our very eyes."

Eleazar nodded glumly, and mechanically continued his dutiful accounting. "Judah," he reported, "has increased from 74,600 to 76,500."

Moses smiled broadly. "They're a good bunch those lads! What did our father Israel say of them? 'The scepter shall not depart from Judah nor the ruler's staff from between his feet, until he comes to whom to it belongs, and to him shall be the obedience of the people.'[21] No wonder God asked me to get them to lead the people in all our wanderings."

Still frowning, Eleazar glumly nodded. "And Zebulon has gone from 57,400 to 60,500."

Now Moses was beaming. "Fantastic!"

---

20. Numb 25:1–3. Beth-Peor was the name of the place where the liaison with Midianites occurred.

21. Gen 49:10

Facing a Glorious Future.

"And Issachar has gone from 54,400 to 64,300. But I better check those numbers. They seem a bit too good to be true."[22]

"Don't bother," admonished Moses, laughing joyfully. "We see the blessing of God before our very eyes! None of the tribes of Judah, Zebulun or Issachar fraternized with those Midianite women. It's powerful proof that choosing God results in blessing, exactly as I've tried to tell the people!"

Just then one of the census men hurried in. "I'm very sorry. We forgot to count that old man over there in the terebinth grove."

Eleazar was about to add him into the tally when Moses raised a cautionary hand. "I think we should go over and visit him, but there's no need to include him in the tally. He's much too old for war."

Eleazar frowned, as he was keen to finish the work, but the other census officials quickly agreed they would like to visit Betsalel, and Joshua led the way. A pleasant walk to a grove of attractive trees made a welcome change from mere counting, important as the results clearly proved to be. As they approached his couch, Betsalel waved to the men. But when they reached him, he appeared to be sound asleep.

Moses went over and touched him, but there was no response. "He's the last of the people counted in the wilderness of Sinai," said Moses. "There's not one left.[23] Most are forgotten, but the legacy of this man shall live. As you all know, God filled him with his Spirit."[24]

No one dared mention that it would actually be Moses who would be the last to die.

Suddenly Joel walked to the head of Betsalel's bed, turned, and faced the group. "Brothers," he began, his now black beard, only lightly grizzled, trembling slightly with emotion. "Let's never forget. Do you remember the day we first met Betsalel? It was that terrible day you lost your family, Assir, but come, stand with me, man!" Assir rapidly moved to Joel's side. "Yes, the day Betsalel called his great disappointment. Kenaz, you come here, too, mate," and Kenaz walked firmly to stand with his friends. "Yes, Kenaz, grandson of Caleb! Remember how you heard the wife of Uri weeping, and your mother told you she thought her son had died? So we were sent to find

22. For these census numbers, compare Numbers Chapters 1 and 26.

23. Numb. 26:64–65. According to Deut 2:14 all men over twenty years at Kadesh Barnea died by the 38th year of the wilderness wandering, before the conquest of the Kings Sihon and Og. To include ideas from Deuteronomy and the census, however, I have extended Betsalel's life a little.

24. Exod. 31:1–11; 35:30

him. Come on, Phinehas, and Jahath, and Chelubai and Obadiah!" Led by the priest Phinehas, in his stately white robe, the men moved to Joel's side.

"I'll never forget that day. You'll remember how we watched Betsalel. Man, he was solid sorrow! We were terrified he really had died! But finally he moved, smiled at us, and invited us to join him to talk about things. Don't know about you, but I was too scared to say no. We were just so pleased we'd found him alive. But think what he has given us. He had no children, and by accident I found out why. So we are his children. We learned about his God, his wonderful God, so let's all pledge to be absolutely loyal, not to Betsalel, but to the God he loved so much! Will you join me in this pledge?"

"Praise God!" cried Moses, "God is good. His mercies endure forever, and ever, and ever!"

"But there's something else," continued Joel, his voice softer. "All that Betsalel helped us understand about God was truly amazing. But he did something else for me. Just before I got married, he had a talk with me. I can see Milcah over there, and I guess I've never told her, but she has Betsalel to thank for our very happy marriage. I pondered what he told me, and tried to do as he said, and it has been wonderful. Milcah, I know you're shy, but would you be willing to come and join me, join us, to give honor to our friend Betsalel?"

The sound of murmuring rippled across the group, as Milcah slowly, blushingly, made her way to Joel's side. Her gown was of delicately woven multicolored natural wool, and her head covering a beautiful blue that complemented her rich auburn hair. When she reached her husband he grinned broadly, and declared, "Anyone wanting to know the secrets for a successful marriage can come and talk to me personally."

A ripple of friendly laughter greeted his offer. When it died away Joel solemnly announced, "And let's promise we'll give ourselves totally to God, Yahweh, to conquer that land for him! Yes, let's do it for Yahweh, not for Betsalel, not for Moses, but for our amazing God who saved us from the slavery of Egypt, and who has brought us to the very border of the Promised Land."

All the men shouted, "Amen!" "With God we can do it!" "We shall be conquerors for Yahweh!" And they bowed their heads in worship.

Betsalel was buried with due ceremony, but without any mourning time as he had requested. "Focus on Canaan," was his mantra under the terebinth tree.

A few days after Betsalel's funeral Moses came to Joshua and Eleazar. "God has called me to meet him up the mountain," he announced quietly. "I'm to go alone. I'm not sure if or when I'll return, but please don't let anyone follow me."

The three men prayed together, then Moses began his solitary journey up Mount Nebo, to the great heights of Pisgah. Eleazar watched the aged leader walk firmly towards his destination. "He's remarkable, considering he's 120 years old!"[25] he exclaimed to Joshua.

When Moses did not return after a week, Joshua and Eleazar knew he had made his last rendezvous with God, and died on the mountain. When the people heard this they spontaneously began a thirty-day time of deep mourning.[26]

But as soon as they had overcome their grief, Joshua immediately had them prepare to cross the River Jordon, and enter Canaan.[27]

The time for God to fulfill Betsalel's dream had finally come.

25. Deut. 34:7
26. Deut 34:1–8
27. Deut 34:9; Josh 1:1–2, 10–11

13

Reflections

B ut Betsalel's story did not end with his death.

In the year 970 BC, 476 years after Israel came out of Egypt and settled in the Promised Land,[1] a royal procession wound its way from Jerusalem, the city of David, to the provincial town of Gibeon in the territory of Benjamin. Solomon, newly crowned as king of Israel, made this pilgrimage to Gibeon because the remnants of the sacred old tabernacle, now nearly half a millennium old, were there. He wanted to obtain divine approval, consolidate his royal authority, and justify his ascension to the throne because he had older brothers contending for the position.[2]

In the courtyard of this ancient tabernacle, seriously decrepit due to neglect more than age, one important thing remained intact, and it was the focus of Solomon's visit. "The bronze altar that Betsalel the son of Uri, the son of Hur, had made was there before the tabernacle of the LORD."[3] This is an amazing testament to the encouraging fact that work done according to God's specifications will last as long as God needs it.

But God's plans can be distorted. The text continues, "And Solomon went up there to the bronze altar before the LORD, which was at the tent

---

1. The fourth year of Solomon has been firmly established as 966 BC, see ESV Study Bible notes, also Andrews Study Bible, on 1 Kings 6:1, which states: "In the 480th year after the children of Israel had come out of the land of Egypt, in the fourth year of Solomon's reign . . . he began to build the house of the Lord." Thus the first year of his reign would have been 476 years after leaving Egypt, and in the year 970 BC.

2. 1 Kings 1:5–53.

3. 2 Chron 1:5

of meeting, and offered a thousand burnt offerings on it."[4] Moses' fear that rituals would overtake the worship of God had indeed occurred. To offer one thousand burnt offerings emphasized devotion to ritual, but was utterly devoid of meaning. Such a display of wealth and extravagance had *never* been asked for by God. JoAnne Davidson describes the repulsion and disgust she experienced a few years ago when she was present in Shechem, Israel, for the yearly Samaritan Passover sacrifice of a lamb, and how suddenly, in the midst of her negative thinking about how a God of love could possibly institute such a gruesome ritual, she realized it powerfully demonstrated just how bad, just how terrible, sin really is.[5] One lamb was enough to show that!

God understood Solomon intended to do what was right, despite his limited understanding. Perhaps Solomon never knew what the prophet Samuel so pertinently told King Saul, "Behold, to obey is better than sacrifice, and to hearken than the fat of rams".[6] But, importantly, the ancient altar was so well constructed that it was still capable of coping with burnt offerings. And the man who made it, the Holy Spirit-filled Betsalel, the son of Uri, the son of Hur, was remembered as its maker.

However, the meaning of the tabernacle services had indeed been seriously eroded by the time Solomon came to the throne. Ritual and dreams of grandeur had overtaken God's plans to share with his people his self-sacrificing love, his long term plans for their salvation, and to encourage their witness to the rest of the world. Misunderstanding still impacts our thinking, leading to hopes and plans that do not elevate God's love, but rather human pride and international contention.

Around A.D.1440 John Lydgate coined the phrase "comparisons are odious."[7] The wisdom of the phrase was repeated by Cervantes, Christopher Marlowe, and John Donne, and Shakespeare gave it his own inimitable twist when he opined that "comparisons are odorous". But comparisons can be instructive, and if the original sanctuary is compared to Solomon's lavish structure, much can be learned. Recognizing that Betsalel's God-given work was intended to make clearer the spiritual understanding of salvation

---

4. 2 Chron. 1:3–6

5. Davidson, JoAnn, "Shaken at Shechem" (2020). Faculty Publications. 3422.https://digitalcommons.andrews.edu/pubs/3422

6. 1 Sam. 15:22

7. https://www.phrases.org.uk/meanings/Comparisons-are-odious.html 3rd August, 2021.

for all God's people, it is vital to remember the focus: God. It is easy to get off track, and think systems, rituals, and buildings have value in themselves, which is what happened with the grand temple built by Solomon.[8] It may seem inappropriate to criticize something as beautiful as the Jewish temples most undoubtedly were, but the tragic fact is they were not the acme of divine perfection, despite having captured an unfortunate and misplaced emphasis in the understanding of prophecy. God allowed both Solomon's and Herod's temples to suffer fiery destruction. The tragedy of the original tabernacle is that it was never destroyed, but simply suffered neglect and abandonment by the very people it was designed to help.

The town of Gibeon, where the ancient bronze altar was situated and where Solomon and his entourage headed, is significant because there, during the conquest of Canaan, God's well-meaning people failed to follow his commands, and made a covenant with Canaanite people who deceived them into believing they came from a faraway country.[9] But God mercifully overruled their mistake, using it as a catalyst for the conquest of much of Canaan, and the means of incorporating the Gibeonites into the community of Israel.[10]

The original tabernacle, whose construction was supervised by Betsalel, had, after the conquest of Canaan, first been erected at Shiloh.[11] Later it was moved to Shechem, a significant town with a tragic history,[12] situated on the plain between Mounts Gerizim and Ebal. Here God, through Moses, specifically asked his people to meet,[13] and here Joshua obediently gathered Israel to remake their covenant with God. The tabernacle was finally, "permanently" pitched at Shiloh (twelve miles south of Shechem, and twenty miles north of Jerusalem) during the times of the Judges,[14] and here young Samuel ministered under the direction of the High Priest Eli.[15] But the disgraceful behavior of the sons of Eli resulted in the capture of

8. Jer 7:1–15; Eze 8:1–18

9. Josh.9:3–27, noting verse 14: "the men . . .did not ask direction from the Lord".

10. Josh. 10:1–43

11. Josh. 18:1, Jer. 7:12

12. Josh. 24:1,25–26. It was near Shechem that Jacob settled after his twenty-year sojourn with his uncle Laban, Gen 33:15–20, but there followed the tragic massacre of the city's inhabitants by Jacob's sons Simeon and Levi after their sister Dinah, Jacob's only daughter, was defiled by Shechem, son of Hamor, prince of the land, Gen 34:1–31.

13. Deut. 27:2–14

14. Judges 18:31

15. 1 Sam.1:3,11, 24–28

the ark by the Philistines,[16] and subsequently (probably during the early part of Samuel's judgeship) the ark-less sanctuary was moved to Gibeon, which became after the conquest of Canaan a Levitical city. Taking the ark into war, as the renegade young priests Hophni and Phinehas did, had a special, but misunderstood, precedent. When Israel conquered Jericho the ark was carried by the priests in an amazing, eerie, procession that marched around the city for seven days. The shout that brought the walls of Jericho down highlighted the fact that this tactically unique victory was due to the presence of God fighting for his people, not to "magical" qualities in the ark.[17] The fact that it was God who brought the victory was emphasized by the command that all plunder, the recognized reward for the victor, was to go into the treasury of the Lord.[18]

After decades of wandering, during most of the reigns of Kings Saul and David, about fifty years, the ark was finally brought to Jerusalem by David.[19] But the whole symbolism of the tabernacle was severely damaged by this fragmentation of its parts. However, Solomon hearkened to the *desire* of his father King David, and built a grand, costly, and luxurious temple to replace the ancient tabernacle designed by God. But there was no clear command from God for this temple, merely permission, perhaps similar to the permission given Israel to have a king, something which was not part of God's original plan.[20]

When David first had the idea of building God a "house", after he brought the ark into Jerusalem, God brushed the idea aside, poignantly indicating that he was completely happy with the old tabernacle built under his direction in the wilderness: "Thus says the LORD 'Would you build me a house to dwell in? I have not dwelt in a house since the day I brought up the people of Israel from Egypt . . . but I have been moving about in a tent for my dwelling . . . Did I speak a word to any of the judges of Israel, whom I commanded to shepherd my people, "Why have you not built me a house of cedar?" . . . the LORD declares to you that the LORD will make you a house . . . I will raise up your offspring after you . . . and I will establish his kingdom. . . .I will establish the throne of his kingdom forever."'[21] Clearly

16. 1 Sam.4:1–11
17. Josh. 6:1–21
18. Josh. 6:17–19
19. 2 Sam.6:1–19
20. 1 Sam 8:4–22
21. 2 Sam. 7:1–17

God was happy with the original tabernacle (which did, however, need to be maintained properly by the Levites chosen by God for this duty), and was giving David an encouraging prophetic announcement regarding the future Messiah, the *real* temple of Israel, the *real* house of David. But David either misunderstood (despite what now appears to be a clear prophecy), or ignored it.

Some time after this David sinned by numbering Israel.[22] He was a warrior, and this numbering was clearly for military purposes, which God could not bless. David should have remembered the story of Gideon, when God pared down the army from a militarily respectable 32,000 to a ridiculous 300, less than one per cent of the original force, then effected an amazing victory.[23] Nearer to David's own time and experience was the astonishing victory of Jonathan, who, with just himself and his armor bearer, won the city of Jebus for Israel (which suggests Jerusalem should have been called the city of Jonathan, and not of David![24]). And of course there was David's own famous conquest over Goliath, when God wrought a huge victory for his people through just a boy and his sling.[25]

So David had ample reason to understand that numbers were not what counted with God. But he was human, and we all think bigger is better (usually). David's numbering exercise caused a plague which the prophet Gad told David could be contained if he, David, built an *altar* on the threshing floor of Araunah (or Ornan) the Jebusite.[26] It was on this elevated threshing floor that *David* decided the temple should be built,[27] although fire coming from heaven to consume his sacrifice might suggest the location was acceptable to God. However, fire came from God to consume Elijah's sacrifice on Mount Carmel, but this did not signify any command to build a house for God there.[28] Solomon's temple was built on Mount Moriah,[29] the general location where Isaac was offered for sacrifice.[30] But notably, as God had

22. 1 Chron. 21:1,7

23. Judges 7:2–25

24. 1 Sam.14:1–15

25. 1 Sam.17:1–16, 22–23, 26, 31–54

26. 2 Sam. 24:1–25, 1 Chron. 21:1–30.

27. 1 Chron. 21:28—22:2

28. 1Kings 18:1–39

29. 2 Chron. 3:1

30. Gen 22:2. Notably this is called "the land of Moriah" in Genesis, and is an area rather than a specific mountain peak.

already indicated to David, he preferred to move around in the midst of the people.[31] Of significance are the dramatic prophecies given to Ezekiel, the exiled prophet on the banks of the Babylonian River Chebar, and Daniel in the Babylonian palace, in which God was clearly depicted as mobile.[32] After David's sin of numbering the people, implicit, not explicit, permission to build a house was given.[33] David declared to his son that he had been shown plans from God: "Every part of this plan," David told Solomon, "was given to me in writing from the hand of the LORD," but there is no clear "Thus saith the LORD."[34] However, whilst the record of the building of the wilderness tabernacle gives very frequent mention that construction was carried out according to God's plans,[35] this is never recorded for the building of Solomon's temple. Whilst God's giving instructions to Moses was very public, and two helpers were clearly called by God to lead the construction, the process appears as a very private arrangement between David and his son.

Shaun Nelson presents arguments that suggest David's desire to build a magnificent temple was not an original intention from God, and indicates the whole temple plan was an idea from "David's flesh".[36] Another voice sharing this opinion that the temple was not part of God's plan comes from James Burton Coffman.[37] Solomon's desire to build a temple for God was strongly connected to his desire to build a lavish palace for himself.[38]

Why it never occurred to Samuel, David, or Solomon to restore the old tabernacle according to the very clear specifications in the Torah is a mystery. Perhaps the tabernacle was so dilapidated they thought nothing could restore it to its former glory, because, after all, much of its external

31. 2 Sam 7:4–7

32. Ezek. 1:4–28; Dan 7:9

33. 1 Chron. 21:1—22:1, 7–17, noting verse 22:1, 28:10–20.

34. 1 Chron. 28:19, NLT

35. For example, Exod. 39:7,21,26,29, 31,32,42–43; 40:16,19, 23,25, 27, 29, 32.

36. Nelson, Shaun. "David's Magnificent Temple Built in the Flesh", 2013. Nelson suggests, as I have done, that David either willfully or inadvertently misunderstood God's prophecy, given through the prophet Nathan, that God would provide David with a "house" meaning posterity, and not a physical building.

37. Coffman, James Burton. *The James Burton Coffman Commentary Series: The Historical Books,Commentary on 2 Samuel 7* (Abilene: Abilene Christian University Press, 1974).

38. See 2 Chron. 2:1, 1 King 6:37—7:1, indicating Solomon spent seven years building God's house, but thirteen building his own. Where did his priorities lie?

construction was from soft, fragile, and perishable materials. In fact, although the original tabernacle internally was extremely beautiful, at no time was it *externally* impressive. However, the original instructions in the Torah were clear and should therefore have easily allowed restoration.

Notably, for the construction of Solomon's temple, instead of an Israelite community working cheerfully and enthusiastically together to build the sanctuary as under Betsalel's Spirit-filled leadership,[39] Solomon employed *forced* and *"resident alien"* labor.[40] Instead of a Betsalel and an Oholiab, men filled with the Spirit of God, supervising the construction,[41] Solomon sent to King Hiram, of the Phoenician city of Tyre, to provide a skilled but *foreign* workman to oversee construction.[42] The ancestry of the man sent to oversee the building of the temple is somewhat clouded in mystery. The Second Chronicles account calls him Huram-abi, son of a woman from the tribe of Dan and father from the city of Tyre of the Phoenicians. But in First Kings he is called Hiram, the son of a woman of the tribe of Naphtali who was widow of a man of Tyre. Some see these two names as possibly comparing to both Betsalel and Oholiab, especially as Oholiab came from the tribe of Dan, but this is stretching the connections and the account.[43] What is clear is this man was recommended by foreign King Hiram of Tyre, and not specifically called by God as was Betsalel.

The connection between the King of Tyre and Solomon's temple may have sad significance, as revealed in the book of Ezekiel, and the judgment proclaimed on the polluted temple.[44] Tyre was never a great empire or miliary force, but it was known for its wealth, its proud and widespread trading capacity.[45] There is more than a suggestion that when Solomon turned to Hiram, king of Tyre, for help with building the new temple, he was enlisting the forces of unholy commercial pride. The resulting grandiose but undoubtedly extremely beautiful temple reflected the philosophy, attitude, and spirit of Tyre. Many Christians have seen in the Ezekiel prophecies against the King of Tyre a symbolic representation of the hubris of Satan

---

39. Exod.36:1–2, 39:32, 42–43

40. 1 King 5:13–18, 2 Chron. 2:1–2,17–18.

41. Exod.31:1–11

42. 1 Kings 7:13–14, 2 Chron. 2:3–16.

43. See comments on the above texts in the ESV Study Bible.

44. Ezek. 8:1—9:19; 28:1–19

45. Ezek. Chapter 27.

himself. Thus the King of Tyre's connection with Solomon's temple gives food for sober thought.

Contributions for the temple construction came from King David and the rulers of the people, who gave generously and caused rejoicing among the people.[46] But for the original tabernacle made at the foot of Mount Sinai "they came, both men and women, *all* who were of a willing heart."[47] Solomon used 600 talents of gold just to overlay the Most Holy Place walls,[48] whereas, by contrast, the amount of gold used for the entire wilderness tabernacle was a "mere" twenty-nine talents and 730 shekels,[49] although this was still an incredibly lavish amount from recently liberated slaves.

The extravagant differences between the original tabernacle and the Solomon temple are particularly striking with regard to the furnishings. Instead of the ark of the covenant standing splendidly alone in divine throne-room majesty in the Most Holy Place, two enormous gold-plated olivewood cherubim, each with wing spans of ten cubits, greatly (probably completely!) overshadowed it in Solomon's temple.[50] However, the ark still contained the tables of stone, written by God on Mount Sinai,[51] so not all understanding was lost: the intimate relationship between God's laws and his government was still recognized. Separating the Most Holy and Holy Places, and the temple itself from the peoples' courtyard, were now heavy, ornately carved, gold-plated olivewood doors, and the original soft and beautifully embroidered veils were retained seemingly only as an afterthought, whether on the inside or the outside of the doors is not clear.[52] In the Holy Place, instead of one menorah giving its golden light, now there were ten; instead of one table of showbread, now there were also ten.[53] The original meaning of one great God providing light to the world, and the One God of Israel giving the bread of life is tragically dissipated. The altar

---

46. 1 Chron. 29:1–9

47. Exod. 35:20–29

48. 2 Chron. 3:8. Given that a talent was about 34 Kgs, 600 talents of gold is an incredible amount.

49. Exod. 38:24

50. 1 Kings 6:23–28, 2 Chron.3:10–13.

51. 1 Kings 8:9, 2 Chron. 5:10.

52. 1Kings 6:31–35; 2 Chron. 3:14, 4:22.

53. 1 Kings 7:48–49; 2 Chron. 4:7–8.

of incense is mentioned briefly, again almost as an afterthought.[54] Whether it was the original or another one is not clear.

In the courtyard, which originally featured prominently as the place for the people to bring their sacrificial sin and burnt offerings and meet with the priests, Solomon's new altar for burnt offerings was huge, and so high the people were cut off from its ministry. The one Betsalel built according to God's specifications was five cubits by five cubits by three cubits high,[55] a human-manageable size, but Solomon's altar was twenty by twenty cubits.[56] Worse, this altar was ten cubits high (that is, five meters), necessitating the priests must ascend steps to attend to the offerings, yet God had specifically declared that his people should *not* go up by steps to his altar.[57] Instead of the "laver," or washbasin, made by Betsalel from the bronze mirrors lovingly, selflessly, donated by the women,[58] considerable space is given to describe a large bronze "sea" standing on the backs of twelve oxen, and as an afterthought is added that ten lavers for cleansing of the priests were made.[59] The bronze for this enormous "sea" was obtained from spoils of war by David's battles with Hadadezer, King of Zobah, an area north of Damascus.[60] The design of this "sea" is a tragic but no doubt unintentional reminder of the molten calf incident, although possibly it was intended to be a reminder of the twelve tribes. Instead of one laver for priestly cleansing there were now no less than—yes, ten — large washbasins on wheeled stands, with the inconsequential stands (not the wash basins!) described in incredible detail![61] The capacity of the "sea" was about 44,000 liters, and one wonders how this amount of stagnant water could be kept clean and pure. Everything was grandiose and lavish, yes, at least ten times grander than the original, potent testament to the riches and power of the king who made it all. It has gone down in history as "Solomon's temple". What Betsalel constructed was called, significantly, and simply, "the taber-nacle of the LORD".[62]

54. 1 Kings 7:48, 2 Chron.4:19.

55. Exod. 27:1

56. 2 Chron.4:1. A cubit is approximately 0.5 metre.

57. Exod. 20:26

58. Exod. 38:8

59. 1 Kings 7:23–39, 2 Chron.4:2–6.

60. 1 Chron. 18:3,7–8

61. 1 Kings 7:27–37, 2 Chron.4:6.

62. 2 Chron.1:5

The one positive thing in this account of building Solomon's temple is that God still loved his people. At the dedication ceremony, when Solomon ended his impressive and grand prayer, which admitted that God does not live in buildings constructed by humans,[63] fire came down from heaven, consumed the sacrifices, and the glory of the LORD filled the temple.[64] However, the sacrifices offered at this time were again grandiose, no less than an incredible (and brutal) 22,000 oxen, and 120,000 sheep.[65] These sacrifices were peace offerings which no doubt provided thanksgiving and celebratory food for visiting people.[66] But significantly there were so many sacrifices that the grand new altar could not cope and the courtyard itself (that is, the floor!) was used, a rather undignified, even polluted and unholy picture at this time of celebration, even though Solomon is said to have "consecrated" this area.[67] It is of great significance that later the Prophet Isaiah specifically spoke against this multiplicity of ritualistic sacrifice: "'What to me is the multitude of your sacrifices?' says the LORD. 'I have had enough of burnt offerings of rams and the fat of well-fed beasts; I do not delight in the blood of bulls, or of lambs, or of goats.'"[68] Significantly, the glory of the LORD could only fill Solomon's temple *after* the priests had left it.[69] This is in stark contrast to the dedication of the original tabernacle, when the glory of the LORD filled the sanctuary *before* any services took place.[70]

When the original tabernacle was dedicated, a service that lasted twelve days, there were twelve bulls, twelve rams and twelve lambs for burnt offerings and twelve goats for sin offerings (each day a different tribe presented one of each of these animals). As a total fellowship peace offering over these celebratory twelve days there were, for the entire wilderness congregation (estimated at about two million), twenty-four oxen, sixty rams, sixty goats and sixty lambs, making the *total* number of animals sacrificed thirty-six

63. 2 Chron 6:18

64. 2 Chron. 7:1–3

65. 2 Chron.7:4–5

66. See Lev 3:1–17, 1Kings 8:63.

67. 1 Kings 8:64, 2 Chron. 7:7.

68. Is. 1:11. A pertinent comment on this appears in E. G. White *Life Sketches*: "Had they been obedient and *loved* to keep God's commandments, the multitude of ceremonies and ordinances would *not* have been required," p 200 (emphases supplied).

69. 1 Kings 8:10–11, 2 Chron.7:1–3

70. Exod. 40:33–35. See also Roy Gane, "Sanctuary Principles for the Church Community", *Perspective Digest* Vol. 12, 2007.

bulls/oxen, seventy-two rams, seventy-two lambs, and seventy-two goats, a dramatically smaller and more humane number than at the Solomon temple dedication.[71] After the temple and Solomon's own house were built (significantly, Solomon took seven years to build the temple —Betsalel and his helpers took seven months — but thirteen to build his own house[72]), God again appeared to him saying he would put his name there forever, and would establish David's throne *if* (and that *if* is very important) he and his people obeyed everything God had told them. But God also gave strong (and tragically prophetic) warnings about the dire consequences that would occur if Solomon and the people turned away from God.[73]

The original wilderness-built tabernacle lasted for 480 years, at least until the fourth year of Solomon's reign when he commenced work on his new temple, and the ark of the covenant much longer, until the temple itself was destroyed and the ark disappeared into mystery. The fate of the other furniture of the original tabernacle is unknown, but possibly they too continued until the final destruction of the Solomonic temple. Solomon's temple was completed in 959 BC, seven years after it was commenced in the fourth year of his reign, and destroyed by Nebuchadnezzar in 587 BC, making its lifespan, for all its grandeur, 372 years, a century less than the original wilderness-constructed tabernacle. Thus the ark (and possibly bronze altar, golden table for shewbread, golden altar for incense, and original menorah) that Betsalel constructed according to God's plan lasted a known 850 years.

At the time of the Babylonian captivity both Jeremiah and Ezekiel made strong indictments against temple practices. Jeremiah offered these pertinent words: "Do not trust in these deceptive words, 'The temple of the LORD, the temple of the LORD, the temple of the LORD.'"[74] The prophet continued, "Will you steal, murder, commit adultery, swear falsely, make offerings to Baal and go after other gods that you have not known, and then come and stand before me in this house, which is called by my name and say 'We are delivered'—only to go on doing all these abominations? Has this house, which is called by my name, become a den of robbers in your eyes?'"[75] When Jesus spoke these words at his final cleansing of the temple,

71. Numb.7:1–88.
72. 1Kings 6:38—7:1, 9:10
73. 1 Kings 9:1–9, 2 Chron. 7:11–22.
74. Jer. 7:4
75. Jer.7:9–15

memories of Jeremiah's words and the prophetic implications for temple destruction would have been strong, and it is little wonder that the Jewish establishment hated him for it.[76] Clearly the people were putting their faith in the mere temple building, grand and all as it was, and not the God of that temple. Jeremiah continues, "Go now to my place that was in Shiloh, where I made my name to dwell at first, and see what I did to it because of the evil of my people Israel . . . [T]herefore I will do to this house that is called by my name, and in which you trust, and to the place that I gave to you and to your fathers, as I did to Shiloh." However, it is of encouraging significance that it is Jeremiah who also presents the compellingly beautiful description of the New Covenant that recalls and corresponds to the magnificent self-revelation that God gave to Moses after the tragedy of the molten calf incident.[77]

Knowledge of Yahweh, his true worship, and the corrupted temple is the primary theme of Ezekiel, who wrote from captivity in Babylon. His book culminates in the picture of a gigantic temple clearly built by God and not depicting anything ever built by humans, nor asked to be built by humans.[78] The connection with Exodus is notable in Ezekiel's repeated use of the phrase "and you shall know that I am Yahweh" (at least seventy times),[79] and that the first verse of the last chapter Ezekiel, where the Hebrew wording is exactly the same — "and these are the names" —as words that commence and give the Hebrew name to the book of Exodus: "These are the names (of the sons of Israel)."

After more than seventy years in Babylonian captivity, the people of Israel, now reduced to being Judahites, or Jews, returned to their homeland, carrying as the generous donation of their Persian overlords some, at least, of the temple accessory chattels, but none of the crucial symbolic temple furniture.[80] Ezra records that soon after their arrival they started worship services according to the law of Moses, the man of God.[81] This strongly suggests the people went back to the blueprint to find out what God really wanted, but they were slow to start building a new temple. Not until the prophet Haggai strongly reproved them did things get under way,

---

76. Matt 21:12–17; Mark 11:15–18; Luke 19:45–46.

77. Compare Jer. 31:31–34, and Exodus 34:6–10.

78. Ezekiel chapters 40—48.

79. See for example Exod. 6:7; 7:5,17; 8:22 etc., and Ezek.5:13;6:7,10,13,14 etc.

80. Ezra 1:1–11

81. Ezra 3:1–6

although interestingly Haggai asked the people to gather wood to build the "house" which does not suggest such a grand structure as Solomon's temple.[82] Although the prophecies of Ezekiel must have been known (note for example Ezek. 8:1, 20:1 that refer to elders of the people coming to see Ezekiel) there was clearly no attempt to build a temple according to the gigantic measurements and plan found in Ezekiel 40—48. Obviously these plans were understood at the time as symbolic prophecy; in fact, it would have been physically impossible to apply the Ezekiel temple plans to the topography of the Jerusalem temple site. But even when building did start, once again they depended heavily on foreign expertise and labor.[83] When a ceremony was organized to celebrate the laying of the foundation of the new temple many were strangely disappointed, and old men who remembered the former glory of Solomon's magnificent edifice ruined the event by weeping.[84] It must have been a strangely disturbing occasion. No details about the construction or furniture of this temple are given, but it appears the leaders tried to return to the original plan given by God, and despite opposition,[85] the temple was finally completed. This time all the people celebrated with joy, and the sacrifices offered were much more constrained and more in accordance with God's directions.[86]

A few hundred years later King Herod, to make a name for himself, lavished much effort on "rebuilding" the post-exilic temple. This was the temple Jesus knew, but there is more than a hint of derision and reference to history when Jesus said, "Destroy this temple, and in three days I will raise it up," uttered after his first "cleansing of the temple", when he drove out lucrative money changers and dishonest animal sellers. Initially Jesus' disciples were shocked, distracted by the lavish forty-six-year building activities of King Herod. "The Jews then said, 'It has taken forty-six years to build this temple, and will you raise it up in three days? But he spoke of the temple of his body. When therefore he was raised from the dead his disciples remembered that he had said this; and they believed the scripture and the word which Jesus had spoken."[87] When Jesus again "cleansed" the temple at the end of his ministry, he referred to the words of both Isaiah

82. Haggai 2:2–9
83. Ezra 3:7
84. Ezra 3:10–13
85. See Ezra chapters 4, 5, and 6.
86. Ezra 6:16–18
87. John 2:13–22

and Jeremiah, saying the desecrators had made the temple a "den of rob-bers" instead of a "house of prayer".[88] Jesus' references to the temple being himself are highly significant. He did not come as the grand, impressive, hoped-for majestic "king" as befitted the ornate and grand temple, but, like the original tabernacle, hid his divinity under the "animal skins" of an ordinary human being.

This is a powerful lesson for God's contemporary people. We need to get back to the simplicity of God's plans, what his Word truly teaches, remove all our lavish embellishments in worship and doctrine, and see our God, our Creator and Redeemer, as he has revealed himself to us in all his beauty of holiness. God wants to dwell, tabernacle, among us[89] which was of course what Jesus came to do.[90] Significantly, God's willingness to come and dwell in a tent made of animal skins, rather than in a lavish hewn-stone temple, is poignant commentary on the whole ministry of Jesus Christ, Immanuel, God with us.[91] "Christ Jesus, though he was in the form of God, did not count equality with God a thing to be grasped, but emptied himself, acting the form of a servant, being born in the likeness of men. And be-ing found in human form he humbled himself and became obedient unto death, even death on a cross."[92]

After the death of Jesus the deacon Stephen, in his powerful personal defense directed towards his Jewish executioners, clearly recognized there was no further need of a temple. He stated: "Our fathers had the tabernacle of witness in the wilderness, as he appointed, instructing Moses to make it according to the pattern that he had seen, which our fathers, having received it in turn, also brought with Joshua into the land possessed by the Gentiles, whom God drove out before the face of our fathers until the days of David, who found favor before God and asked to find a dwelling for the God of Jacob. But Solomon built him a house. However, the Most High does not dwell in temples made with hands, as the prophet says: 'Heaven is my throne, and earth is my footstool. What house will you build for me?' says the LORD, or what is the place of my rest? Has my hand not made all these things?'"[93]

88. Luke 19:46, Is 56:7, Jer 7:11.
89. Exod. 25:8
90. John 1:14
91. Is 7:14
92. Phil. 2:5–8
93. Acts 7:44–50

Christ's death on the cross gives eternal salvation to Christians; it is our hope for everything. It was the fulfillment of all the symbolic sacrifices on the bronze altar. But it is easy to fail to appreciate the rest of the tabernacle imagery and symbolism, and forget the prayer Jesus taught. We have a new identity, a new allegiance; we are part of the kingdom of God. To accept the sacrifice of Jesus without realizing that as his followers we are committed to doing everything his way, to seeing things from his perspective, is a tragedy.

> Our Father, who is in heaven, Hallowed be your name.
> *Your* kingdom come,
> *Your will be done,* on earth as it is in heaven.
> Give us this day our daily bread;
> And forgive us our debts, as we forgive our debtors.
> Lead us not into temptation,
> But deliver us from evil
> For *yours is the kingdom*, the power and the glory,
> Forever, and ever, Amen. (Matt.6:9–13, margin, emphases supplied.)

God's kingdom has not yet come to this earth as it is in heaven. God's will is not yet being done on this earth. We need to enlarge our understanding and move beyond the incredible sacrifice of Jesus Christ our Passover, our courtyard bronze-altar offering, into the second Holy and third Most Holy apartments.

The symbolism of the courtyard and Passover has been fulfilled. The second apartment Holy Place, the Feast of Pentecost, the empowerment by the Holy Spirit, are being fulfilled. We are now on the doorstep of the time of Yom Kippur and entry into the Most Holy Place, with its scary picture of judgment, but also its wonderful promise of the ultimate banishment of sin and suffering. Then we can look forward to the time of *Succoth*, the final Feast of Tabernacles, when we can rejoice forever in the true Promised Land, the new heavens and new earth.

A tragic mistake many sincere Christians make is to focus attention on the rebuilding of a temple in Jerusalem. Not only does this desecrate the image of Jesus as the temple, and dishonor his momentous sacrifice by re-introducing the now completely obsolete animal sacrifices, but it distracts from the important prophetic teachings of the tabernacle services. The judgment time of Yom Kippur is undoubtedly frightening, but the associated and vitally important message of the banishment of sin forever is extremely good news that needs to be shared.

Ezekiel's vision of the new temple has great significance. In chapter 47 the strange picture of a tiny stream issuing from below the threshold of the temple is presented (miraculous, because on Jerusalem's temple mount there was no supply of fresh water, the reason for Solomon's huge bronze reservoir). This stream quickly becomes a large river that nourishes some clearly miraculous celestial fruit trees: "On the banks and both sides of the river grow all kinds of trees for food. Their leaves do not wither, nor their fruit fail, and they bear fresh fruit every month because their water flows from the sanctuary, and their leaves [are] for healing."[94] This correspondence to the New Jerusalem of Revelation and its river and tree of life is remarkable,[95] and shows Ezekiel's vision is not for an earthly temple. The final words of Ezekiel's vision are most illuminating and comforting: "The name of the city from that time on shall be, The LORD is there."[96] The correspondence to John the Revelator's heavenly New Jerusalem, "And I saw no temple in the city, for its temple is the Lord God Almighty and the Lamb,"[97] is remarkable. Perhaps the most amazing picture of the temple of God is found in Isaiah 57:15: "For thus says the high and lofty One, who inhabits eternity, whose name is Holy: I dwell in a high and holy place, and also with him who is of a contrite and humble spirit, to revive the spirit of the humble, and revive the heart of the contrite." God still wants to dwell with us! For eternity!

Just prior to Ezekiel's beautiful words promising God's eternal presence are what appear boring Israelite gate arrangements that do not match the original Israelite camp layout. The careful organization of the Israelite tribal encampment is now muddled up.[98] On the north side gates for the rival leaders Reuben and Judah, plus "disinherited" Levi are waiting for the now peaceful family to enter. East gates are for the tribes of Joseph, Benjamin, and amazingly, Dan, their once hurting and envious half-brother—what better picture of restored harmony can be given! On the south the once rebellious Simeon marches in beside formerly loyal Issachar and Zebulun. And finally the lowly sons of the serving girls, Gad, Asher, and Naphtali are united and enter from the west.[99] Reminiscent of the Israelite camp,

94. Ezek. 47:1–12
95. Rev. 22:1
96. Ezek. 48:35
97. Rev. 21:22
98. See Num 2:1–31
99. Ezek. 48:30–35

the subtle changes in organization and relationship can only occur if God, Immanuel, has indeed filled all his people with his Spirit, and they have new hearts full of God's love. [100] Like the temple prophecy itself, these references to the tribes of Israel, most of whom have long disappeared into the fog of history, are symbolic of the totality of God's people down through the centuries, and the transformation his Spirit can make in them.

And in that wonderful earth made new imagine what it will be like to meet with Moses and Betsalel, all the patriarchs and prophets of old, like Ezekiel, and of course Jeremiah and Isaiah and others, martyrs through the ages, all God's saved and triumphant people.

Best of all, we will be there with God himself, with Jesus Christ our Saviour, for all eternity. What joy it will be!

"The Spirit and the Bride say, 'Come.' And let him who hears say, 'Come.' And let him who is thirsty come, let him who desires take the water of life without price." Rev 22:17.

The dream of Betsalel will be reality.

---

100. Ezek. 36:26–38

Bibliography

Adkins, Lesley and Roy. *The Keys of Egypt: The Race to Read the Hieroglyphs*. HarperCollins, London. 2000.

Alter, Robert. *The Five Books of Moses: A Translation with Commentary*. W.H. Norton, New York. 2008

Baker, David L. *Two Testaments One Bible: The Theological Relationship Between the Old and New Testaments*. Apollos. Nottingham, England. 2010.

Beale, G.K. "The Temple and the Church's Mission." *New Studies in Biblical Theology #17*, IVP. 2004.

Biblia Hebraica Stuttgartensia Parsed Bible, Olive Tree online version.

Blackburn, W. Ross. *The God Who Makes Himself Known: The Missional Heart of the Book of Exodus*. Intervarsity, Downers Grove, IL 2012.

Bork, Paul, *The World of Moses*. Southern Publishing Association, Nashville, TN. 1978.

Bruckner, James K. *New International Biblical Commentary: Exodus*. Hendrickson Peabody, MA. 2008.

Chambers, Oswald, *My Utmost for His Highest*. There are several published versions.

Childs, Brevard. *Exodus: A Commentary*. SCM, London.1974.

Davidson, JoAnn. "Shaken at Shechem" (2020). Andrews University Faculty Publications. 3422. https://digitalcommons.andrews.edu/pubs/3422

Davidson, R. M. *Typology in Structure: A Study of Hermeneucal Structures*. Andrews University Seminary Doctoral Dissertation Series 2, Berrien Springs, MI. 1981.

Doukhan, Jacques B. *The Mystery of Israel*. Review and Herald. 2004.

———. Editor. *Seventh-day Adventist International Bible Commentary, Genesis*. Pacific Press, Nampa, ID. 2016.

Dybdahl, Jon L. *The Abundant Life Bible Amplifier: Exodus*. Pacific Press, Boise, ID. 1994.

Enns, Peter. *The NIV Application Commentary: Exodus*. Zondervan, Grand Rapids, MI. 2000.

Evans, John, F. *You Shall Know That I Am Yahweh: An Inner-Biblical Interpretation of Ezekiel's Recognition Formula*. Pennsylvania State University Press, University Park, PA, 2019.

Fretheim, Terrence E. *Exodus Interpretation: A Bible Commentary for Teaching and Preaching*. John Knox, Louisville KN. 1991.

Gane, Roy E. *NIV Application Commentary Series, Leviticus and Numbers*, Olive Tree online version.

———. *Altar Call*, digital version

———. "Sanctuary Principles for the Church Community". Perspective Digest, 2007

BIBLIOGRAPHY

Gowan, Donald E. *Theology in Exodus: Biblical Theology in the Form of a Commentary.* Westminster John Knox, Louisville, KN. 1994.

Heschel, Abraham Joshua. *The Sabbath.* Farrar, Straus and Giroux, New York. 1951

Jacob, Benno. *The Second Book of the Bible: Exodus.* Translated by Walter Jacob. KTAV, Hoboken, NJ. 1992.

Janzer, J. Gerald. *Exodus.* Westminster John Knox, Louisville, KN. 1997.

Josephus. *Complete Works.* Kregal Publications. Grand Rapids, MI. 1964.

Nichol, Francis D. Editor. *Seventh-day Adventist Bible Commentary, Volume 1.* Review and Herald, Washington DC. 1976.

Parker, Lois M. *Princess of Two Lands.* Southern Publishing Association, Nashville, TN. 1975.

Peterson, Eugene. *Working the Angles: The Shape of Pastoral Integrity.* William Eerdmans, Grand Rapids, MI. 1987.

Pfeiffer, Charles F. *Egypt and the Exodus.* Baker, Grand Rapids MI. 1964.

Robertson, O. Palmer. *The Christ of the Covenants.* Baker, Grand Rapids, MI. 1980.

Rodriguez, A.M. *Sanctuary Theology in the Book of Exodus.* AUSS24, 1986.

Sach, Andrew, and Alldritt, Richard. *Dig Even Deeper: Unearthing Old Testament Treasure.* Intervarsity, Nottingham, England. 2010.

Sailhammer, J. "The Mosaic Law and the Theology of the Pentateuch." *Westminster Theological Journal* #53, pp241-261.

Sarna, Nahum. *Exodus.* JPS Torah Commentary, Philadelphia, PA. 1991.

White, Ellen G. *The Story of Patriarchs and Prophets, As Illustrated in the Lives of Holy Men of Old.* Pacific Press, Mountain View, CA. 1958

Wright, C.J.M. *The Mission of God: Unlocking the Bible's Grand Narrative.* IVP Nottingham, England. 2006.